THIS IS ME

EMMA NICHOLS

Other books by Emma Nichols

To keep in touch with the latest news from Emma Nichols
and her writing please visit:

www.emmanicholsauthor.com
www.facebook.com/EmmaNicholsAuthor
www.twitter.com/ENichols_Author

Thanks

Without the assistance, advice, support and love of the following people, this book would not have been possible.

Bev, Valden, Kim, and Sam. Thank you for reading my manuscript and giving candid feedback. You weren't expecting this from me any more than I was. I love that you were blown-away, flabbergasted, and appreciated this as my best work yet. I hope this beautiful love story will touch others as it touched you. x

Mu. Cracking cover again. Thank you for your support and love. x

Nicci Robinson, Global Wordsmiths. Thank you. Thank you. Thank you. You promised to edit through my voice and delivered exactly that. Your guidance was spot on and has enhanced this work to achieve the best it could be. The words will now be released and speak for themselves. x

To my loyal readers and followers. This work is different from anything I have written. It is the best book yet. Please don't raise your expectations too high though, eh? :-) I hope this story touches your heart as it did mine in the writing of it.

With love, Emma x

Dedication

For women who love with all their heart

x

1.

We stare at each other across the plastic round table in the cheap café you hate on the high street. One pound fifty a cup. I think that sums up a fundamental difference between us. Extravagance is the light that guides your lost soul, provides comfort, and the illusion of security. My needs are simple. I want for nothing. Material things, money, status: these things matter not to me. Your skin is ashen, taut around your jaw, your lips an almost perfect straight line. Heavy lids fight to darken the world in front of them. How did that world become me?

Your dark eyes hold me with the look of an indoctrinated soldier. It's a wired, insane kind of focus. I've seen it before. I know if you had a weapon in your hand, I would experience the intense rush of adrenaline flood my muscles. Instead, my blood runs cold. You raise a hand. I flinch. It's an instinctive response, but it doesn't serve us. You pinch the bridge of your nose, return your hand in a clenched fist to the table. Your lips twitch as if you have something to say. I wait. Picking at the skin around your thumb, your lips settle again into the comfort of that straight line. There is no rational argument that can compete with the depth of your emotion. None. I've tried many times. It's locked in you, in me, in us now.

The physical distance across the table is too narrow. Maybe no distance will ever be sufficient to stop the pain ricocheting, being batted effortlessly back and forth between us. We are both guilty, of course. These things are never one-sided though you seem to cast blame effortlessly with a well-practised whip of your right wrist. You feel I play the blame game, but that's just projection, isn't it? You wear vulnerability like a comfortable jacket in the purple shadows under your eyes too. But there's more to you than that. More to the both of us, I believe. You've said you believe in us, but I wonder if you believe in the reality of us, who we are, or rather the illusion you created. There has to be a better world than that which delivers nothing but disappointment, doesn't there?

Your chest struggles to expand with the air you suck in through your nose. You don't even motion to speak. I don't know whether that's just because your teeth are clamped, paralysed with intensity, or there are really no words to say that will change the course of events.

I feel stuck too. Wounded. Confused. The fact that we're in this place again eats away at me, drives me to frustration, renders me powerless and devoid of thought. My mind closes down. It's protection, I know that, but I can't stop it. My world closes in before my eyes. I'm struggling to process even the simple, routine stuff at work. I resent that. I resent that a lot. I need my mind to function effectively, and you take that from me. There's no achievement in this stalemate, but we both thrive when we feel our actions are adding value. I don't know where to start any conversation with you. My head is filled with an inexplicable sense of nothingness. Blocked irritation seeps through every pore.

2

I know if I say anything right now I will shout. I will appear aggressive, even though I'm not like that. I don't want to be that person who has to shout to be heard. I already feel misunderstood, and I'm not giving you the ammunition you've used against me before. I want to grab you by the shoulders, shake some sense into you. I imagine you want to do the same to me too. I want to say, "It's over." I need to see you react in some way, you see. I need to know that you care about me. I want free of this pain, the struggle between us. I wonder whether we have always been on a destructive cycle. Have we always been broken?

I say nothing. I'm waiting for an apology but not for the reason you think. The more I hold the thought of needing you to acknowledge your unjustified jealousy, the tighter the pressure becomes in my head, squeezing between my eyes, clamping my jaw, gritting my teeth just like yours. Is sorry so fucking hard to say?

You are a fighter. Of course, sorry is a difficult word. It's an admission that demonstrates weakness, you think. I disagree. I too know what it's like to fight, remember? A different kind of war to yours, I accept. In my experience of doing battle we knew who to trust. We knew whose side we were on. Maybe that's part of the problem. I know who the real enemy is, I know how to fight. And I don't back down easily in the face of the truth—my truth, you'll argue. I've served in Afghanistan, seen death of the cruellest kind, watched helpless as the life drained from innocents taken before their time. You know, guilt doesn't change the look in a man's eyes when he knows his turn is coming either. Abject fear looks the same in us all. I've only ever seen one soldier filled with blind determination to the end, a true believer in something far better waiting for him on the other side. Maybe he was right, but at what cost to the world? I think fear is a guide that keeps us grounded and able to live together. Without the fear of death, and with fanatical beliefs such as he had, there is no level of destruction men like him are not capable of delivering on the world. No sanctions, no threats can ever pull them into line. They have the ultimate power. Self-sacrifice. He was free, but in the most dangerous way to our humanity. We cannot achieve absolute safety in a world where men will give their lives so willingly for a cause that is beyond the realms of this existence.

I know I need to live. Here, now. I have no desire to fight with you. Live, not exist. The stalemate persists in your unbroken glare across the void that won't shift. You'll try and hold out against me, but it's *me* who's angry with *you* so my stamina will win out this time. Deep down, in the places you don't acknowledge exist, in those places, you know it. Guilt saps the strength behind any argument, you know?

Your left eye starts to twitch, and you brush at it with sharp movements. Inside I'm smiling, because you're pissed at your body giving you away. It softens my frustration for a moment but then I get back to my mission. The barriers to forgiveness go up, shutting out the potential for us to move forward yet again. I'm not ready for that. I need an acknowledgement that you take responsibility for this latest blow-up. I'm not hopeful, because you're in fight-mode, and you've lost sight of who the enemy is or what the battle is really about.

You should probably know that your body always gives your thoughts and feelings away. Your story is written in the subtle creases of your fair skin, the sadness behind your deep blue eyes that only sparkle when you feel guilty. The defensive posturing comes through in the over-zealous confidence, the clipped tone in your voice, and the certainty with which you speak about topics you've never studied.

When did you stop laughing? Anger rises in you like a serpent at just the thought of being wrong. Or is it just that you don't want *me* to be right? You wear your broken heart on your sleeve. It bleeds proudly and profusely for all to see, should they really want to look. You hope they won't watch you too closely though, don't you? No one is permitted beneath the veneer. Did anyone tell you that your charade is cracked from the quaking and crumbling inside you? I think you sense its demise in your increasing vulnerability. That shit comes with age too. Some talk about a mid-life crisis. You know, that point in time when we look at our lives and wonder what the fuck it's all been about. We try to see value in our achievements and realise none exist. The future looks like death, and our mind wants to live anywhere but where we now find ourselves. It's tough deriving a sense of worth through the "never-enough" lens though, isn't it? You know the grass isn't greener on the other side of the fence, and yet your side is too barren to sustain life. You're fucked.

There *is* strength in vulnerability. Don't you know that?

Life is unjust, unfair. The child in us knows this to be true. Why do we fight it as adults? War serves no one, not really. And yet it happens the world over. Maybe it always will. I think it's because we're human beings, some with a primal urge to win especially at the cost of others. I've never subscribed to that mindset, but I've known people who do. You see the traits clearly in our political leaders, in those who run the big businesses. Where power is at stake, human dignity is hard to find. It's an ugly world in that regard. Destructive. Divisive. It takes mental strength to concede, to allow another to win when you think you're right. That's the nature of true power: working out which are the most important battles to fight. Not everyone and everything is deserving of the scrap. I am *not* the enemy. We are on the same side. Why is it so difficult for you to believe that? You fear the emotional pain, I understand that. Who doesn't? Physical pain is easier to grasp, you know that too. It's tangible. We're more comfortable relating to a broken arm than a broken heart. The inner pain and suffering go unnoticed with a functioning addict like you, doesn't it? It has a place to hide beneath your sharp intellect and brilliantly creative mind. We had military decorations to show the world that we had fought, suffered, and died in the name of a cause greater than ourselves. What scars mark your chest in recognition of your suffering? I sense the leaded dullness between us at times like these, with you driving me away, trying to provoke a reaction that doesn't come naturally for me. I don't respond well to threat, you know that. Never have done. I guess that comes with being a strong woman. Like you, hostility raises the hackles, and I dig my heels in. I feel my nostrils flare, the fire expanding in my chest. It's not a feeling of anger. It's an insult.

Is there a way back for us?

2.

I hadn't wanted to go to the workshop. I was feeling pissed at the fait accompli that had been issued by the security agency. Yes, I'd seen death, a lot, and when my mum up and died suddenly it damn near broke my heart, but I know how to handle loss. I can compartmentalise it, you see. Stick it in a box and shove it on a shelf in my mind. A colleague recommended the course to me after we lost a client in an assassination. Your course. I wasn't convinced, but I had a procedural box that needed ticking. It wasn't you. I didn't know you from Adam. Cognitive Behavioural and Effective Therapy. I'd never heard of it. I wasn't feeling depressed, angry, or guilty. I'd done all that I could to save him. I couldn't see the value of being lectured to, of reinstalling the moment in my psyche. To what end?

Hindsight is a wonderful thing, and I guess I wear bereavement as you wear vulnerability. A cloak of comforting invisibility. We're the same in that way, aren't we? Maybe that was part of the attraction for me back then. You didn't see me as I saw you. You stepped into the room at a point in time when I didn't really care whether I lived or died. I had no reason to exist. This life spent in isolation was pointless. I had no real friends to drink with, no lover to go home to, no family.

As I watched you look at the expectant faces around the room, my thoughts gathered pace and tumbled clumsily.

There was a hardness in your eyes that was difficult to define. A shield perhaps? I was hooked. You had me intrigued. Did you come into this life with profound sadness or had you learned it? What were you, thirty years old, twenty-eight maybe? It was clear you'd experienced more years than you'd lived, carried the weight of the world on those strong shoulders of yours. I scanned the group: their eyes were on you. They looked desperate, hoping, seeking. You took to the stage with practiced confidence. I took to wondering what made you tick with intense curiosity.

The theory is, if a behaviour is conditioned, it can be changed, you said. But if it's genetic we're pretty much stuck with it. Bottom line, I guess, is that if we're destined to be five-foot-six-inches tall, there's little we can do to change that fact. I'm still not sure how it works, where conditioning meets genetics. What makes one person more willing and able to forgive and forget than another? How is it that someone can be too stubborn and fearful to live and the next person so laissez-faire and devil-may-care? I'm not so sure about that at all.

My point is, it dawned on me then that I wasn't thinking about anyone else in that moment. Not my ex. Not my mom. Not the other people in the room. Just you. I was looking at you and thinking about your dark eyes, your distant gaze, the world locked inside your head. Was I delusional to think I might be able to get inside your mind, take the sadness away, and replace it with kindness and love? Was I attracted to *you*, or did I only see the victim that needed rescuing? I think my pain met yours in a fleeting glance that passed between us.

You were clueless, and I had to work hard for you to see me as different to the rest of the people on the course. I wasn't like the others. I wasn't a victim. I was an ex-soldier who had no desire to fight, no real cause to recognise a purpose or meaning to my life. I hadn't realised I needed those things to feel alive. Little did I know then that you would soon become my cause, my reason to fight. You were to become my reason to live.

Brashness, even aloofness, can be alluring especially with a smile that transforms the energy in a room. You have the kind of smile that entices people to trust in you. It radiates, captivates, expresses optimism. You believed that each one of us could heal from the trauma that afflicted our lives. You drew us into your web, enthralled us with your ideology, and created a vision of a brighter future free from emotional pain. Unquestioning, we believed you. We wanted to, because our lives were train wrecks. What we really wanted was for our partners, our wives, our husbands to be like you. But they weren't. They'd long since stopped trying to meet our needs, barely able to cope with dealing with their own.

I watched you blossom during that first session. Animation suits you. You opened up just enough for your audience to feel you truly cared. You *did* care, I'm sure. You have a gift. You give people passion, a sense of belonging. You re-engage them with their desire to become that which they lost somewhere on the journey of life, probably at the point that things had become difficult. When resources were scarce, when energy waned. I watched you in action from apart from the group, because that's where I like to be, on the outside looking in, taking everything in. You couldn't see me, but I saw you. I may not have been trained as you were with your degrees and doctorate, but I've experienced life. People, pain, love. Passion, chaos, clarity. I've seen *beyond* that which binds us to this earthly reality. I've seen that which exists beyond consciousness.

At the end of the first day when you approached me, you definitely swaggered. Your gaze was as guarded as it had been, your smile sweet and alluring. You removed yourself from the group who had ignited in your presence, approached the bar, and ordered a drink. The barman eyed you up and down. He lingered at your breasts pressed tightly into the black T-shirt. You wore black jeans tight around your narrow hips, your long legs encased in knee-length black boots. I didn't know that was your trademark. The black clothing. The black boots. Skinny, tight jeans. I get it now. I wore a uniform too, but mine was bottle green. I understand what that feels like. There's strength in uniformity: a sense of belonging, of solidarity. The black has a different meaning. Arabs who wear black do so because of their culture. Black is your culture too. I think you chose it so you don't stand out from the crowd, especially here in London where bold colours aren't our native norm. The suits bustling their way to towering, grey buildings hold their black umbrellas aloft in prayer to the dark grey clouds that threaten overhead. And even when the sun shines, we're still a black, blue, and grey kind of nation, aren't we? It's so easy to hide, to blend in with the rest. To remain unseen. It's a shame really. Oranges and golds really work with your pale skin tones. I think if you went to one of those fashion people they would choose very different clothes for you. But, the desire for anonymity, protection, and invisibility are such powerful drivers, aren't they?

Fascination locked me into your world, as if I had no choice but to wonder about you. I wanted to know about the shadows that haunted you. I'd seen tenderness, hints of a gentle, loving heart. But when you looked at me, you didn't see *me*. Professional interest drove you. You wanted to know my pain, that was all. I wanted you to know yours. Looking back, perhaps that was a kind of battle between us. I didn't realise it at the time, but I'd already flouted the boundaries between client and therapist. I wanted to heal your pain as much as you wanted to heal mine. Maybe my thinking was deluded. I only became your client so that I could find out more about my future lover. As if it was set, as if us being together was pre-ordained. I didn't need therapy. I just knew I wanted to see you again. And that time couldn't come soon enough.

*

People have always gravitated towards you when you smile, you know? Over the years, warmth has pulsed achingly through my heart observing their adoration of you. Yet, behind that beautiful blue caress and your bright, white sparkling smile, you hunker down, embroiled in the sadness that resides in the deepest, darkest corners of your mind. In the kaleidoscope you are the centre point. The black hole. Stilled. I sit on the outside, observing. We are opposites, and opposites attract. There's a fine line between pleasure and pain. They are clichés, I know, but they're born from truths that have held over hundreds and thousands of years. I think they merge, otherwise joy and awe wouldn't bring tears or puncture our heart as they often do. Sadness sits at the surface of your world and runs deeper than the dead sea. Unrelenting, the parasite feeds off your soul. Who was I to think I might be able to influence that? Happiness isn't for you, is it? Instead, you thrive on hiding behind the fortitude that has become your ally. You had to learn to be tough, didn't you? You had to, to withstand the constant nibbling at your very being.

It's taken me a few years, but that's what I worked out about you. Am I wrong? And here's the rub. You want to be noticed. You need to be noticed. It's how you feel loved. It's the perfectionist in you, the creative artist in need of recognition. But being seen also scares you shitless. Why? Because if you're noticed, they'll find out about you, won't they? Your secret will be out. That's how fear works. Secrets destroy potential. They diminish your power. Secrets keep you locked in mediocrity, in inadequacy from which you can never escape. That's real "stuck-ness." That from which you need to hide will eventually consume you. Worse than that, the fallout destroys those you love. Collateral damage is costly. I didn't know about your secret back then though. I didn't know about your past. But we all have one. We're not so different, you and me, beneath it all.

13

Is that why we're sitting staring at each other with nothing to say? Tight lipped, fierceness our only defence. You're a fighter still. I'm struggling with the battle. I don't have the will or the energy to engage in combat any more. I learned the futility of it a long time ago. No one really wins.

Did you know I've been working on acceptance? A lot of people will tell you it's not possible, or they'll argue and say, why should they be the ones to accept when others don't? Acceptance is passive. Acceptance is weak. I've heard it all. Those people don't get it, and that's fine. I don't care about them.

I care about you.

I love you.

I see your pain. I feel your pain.

I always have.

3.

Your office in London is nice. Modern with cleanly painted walls, it has a large potted plant in the corner of the room, an old-fashioned, highly polished desk made of dark wood, a black leather two-seater couch, and one of those old handset phones. The classic décor combined with the modern surprises me. As it spills into my glass, the water cooler gurgles aggressively, as if cursing its place amongst those relics. The new and old competing for a place in history. The contrast doesn't work for me, the water cooler belongs outside the room. I don't realise this is a metaphor for you, your thoughts—the old and the new. You move slowly when you hand me the cup. You ease into the director's chair behind your desk, open your pad, and pick up your pen.

"How can I help you?" you ask.

My heart seems to breathe, and the softness inside me starts to gently vibrate. How did you defuse me in that way? I had imagined therapy would be like going into battle, with both sides vying for supremacy over the other, trying to divine secrets and establish dominance through intellect. This is nothing like the feeling one has when going to war. That's a harsh, pounding sensation that grips, and twists, and sends your mind into sharp focus. I try not to smile, but I think something in my eyes must give me away, because you break eye contact. A part of me feels satisfied that I touched you in some small way. I sit up in the seat and sip at the chilled water.

"I don't know," I say. And, I really didn't know. I couldn't tell you specifically why I was there, what I wanted from you. You tease your lips with your tongue as you look away. Do you know how sensual that feels to me, that you've given yourself away already? They're so kissable. It's been a while for me. I can't remember exactly when it was I had last kissed someone. That thought reminds me.

"My ex," I say. The word is out of my mouth before my brain had really processed the question properly. You need an answer from me. Something, anything would do.

"Tell me about your ex," you say.

I can't think of anything to say for a long moment. "She kicked me out." I watch you closely. I don't miss the subtle flicker of muscle movement around your right eye. Others might have. I'm surprised you hadn't realised I was gay. Or maybe you were surprised at my ex's actions.

"How do you feel about that?"

The archetypal question. I shrug. I didn't feel anything. I look toward the window. I'm not avoiding eye contact with you. I can see how you might consider my behaviour in that way, but I always look away when I'm thinking. Clarity comes more easily, and I'm trying to find an emotion I can label and tell you about. My mind is a kind of blank, not in a dark way, just a seeking and can't find kind of way. "I don't feel anything," I say.

You stare at me with those unseeing eyes. You roll your tongue around your teeth then sip at your drink. You're finding it hard to process your thoughts, aren't you? I'd reached into you at the training day, hadn't I?

You scribble something on the paper, though what could have been of interest in what little I had said was a mystery to me. Perhaps you were writing something about your own feelings. You grip the pen tightly and press firmly when you write, don't you? I don't take notes of my thoughts. I guess we're different like that.

"Nothing?"

Your eyes open a fraction further, and the pitch of your voice is slightly higher. I feel the weight of the air lift as it flows from my lungs. I want to help you to help me. "Angry," I say, then wish I hadn't used that emotion. I'd only said angry, because I knew it was a big part of the grief cycle and that was what I should've been feeling. I don't feel angry about anything really. I never have. I should have been reacting badly to the rejection, hurting, fighting, shouldn't I? Truth was, I didn't feel rejected. I didn't feel sad, disappointed, or frustrated. I didn't even feel shitty or guilty, though maybe I should have felt all of those things.

It was my fault after all. At least, that's what *she* had said to me. *I* was to blame for *her* having the affair. I'd asked how? *She* had said it was because I didn't show her enough affection, that I didn't love or care about her, that I was never around. That much was true. I could only get home infrequently especially when I was serving in Afghan.

It wasn't like she hadn't known that would be the case when we got together. She bragged about me to her friends at first, the spontaneous, unpredictable life, the sex, the

17

thrill. But then something shifted between us. It was around the time she knew I was going to be dishonourably discharged. We argued about nothing a lot. She was furious with the injustice of the military might. I was blithe, accompanied my emotionless indifference with a "shit happens" shrug, and that pissed her off even more. I should fight the system, she said. No honourable lesbian fights *this* system, I said. You know the rules when you sign up. If you get caught, game over. It's cruel, harsh, and it isn't right, but it's the way it works. I signed a contract. I broke the rules. Hands up.

We talked about me moving in, but she seemed reticent. The first week everything was fine. It was like being on a leave break. By the end of the first month we were barely speaking. Three months in, and we weren't having sex. She was going out with her mates, and I was working as a bodyguard to the Al Harar's boys in London. My new work kept me away from home, travelling a lot, and we drifted apart. I didn't miss her, I didn't miss home, and she barely knew I existed.

She tried to tell me the affair had been a recent thing but in my gut, I knew she'd been at it with this particular bird for a year or more. There had been others too. The signs were always there. My calls home failing to connect, our clipped conversations, the exaggerated excitement in her voice when talking about the latest night out with friends. You can always tell when someone's cheating on you, if you dare to look.

I'd adjusted and moved on. It hadn't been right between us. We were destined to fail. We'd gone from spending the odd weekend, or sometimes a week, together to full-time living in a rental too small to accommodate her detest of me and my ambivalence toward her. We were two lives converging in a time and space in which neither of us belonged. I figured life is too short to fight the truth. She seemed happy with her new conquest, and I was happy for her.

I don't tell you all of this of course. It's too early for me to share so much, and for reasons I can't explain I want to see you again.

"Where do you feel the anger, Claire?"

I'm conflicted. My name has rolled off your tongue with such tenderness, I feel it trip across my clit. The anger? Fuck knows *where* I'm supposed to feel that, because it's not an emotion that's familiar to me. "My clit," I say.

You look up from the paper on the desk. It's an odd kind of look, and I'm fighting the fire that's trying to engulf my cheeks. I tell myself I didn't just say that, but it's too late. I can tell by the way your lips twitch upwards you're amused, and by the line that has formed between your eyes, that you're also confused. It strikes me that you're disappointed in me. A sharp sensation grips my chest, then it's gone. You look down at the paper, your shoulders rise and fall, and I can see the white of your knuckles as you write.

"The anger?" you ask, again in a soft tone.

You're still looking down, still frowning. *The anger*. I recall the look on my father's face a long time ago. "Tension in my head," I say. It's the best I can come up with.

"Good."

You nod as if we're getting somewhere. Your tone is silky like honey. I'm wet with a dull ache between my legs.

"What rules has she broken?" you ask.

I'm completely thrown by the question, grappling with sensations that have me wanting to leap across the desk and kiss you. "Rules?"

"When we feel anger it's because someone has broken the rules we hold true for ourselves. What rule or rules did she break?"

I look to the window, searching for an answer. I think you understand that mannerism already, because in my peripheral vision I see you're nodding ever so slightly as you watch me processing the question. If the ex had broken any rules, what would they have been? I'm thrashing, drowning in a web of lies of my own creation. Come on, rules, damn you.

You breathe softly.

"Take your time."

Your words distract me, grab my attention from my ex. Your smile conveys patience and compassion. Your eyes are searching, demanding a response that you can make sense of. You want to help me get over something I'm already done with.

"She was having an affair."

Your eyebrows knit together, and the crevasses between them deepen. "She was having an affair, and she kicked you out?"

My vision closes in on the truth as I look down at the hands in my lap. Should I feel annoyed at her? Did I take the passive option? My friends said I should've taken her to the fucking cleaners. They were more pissed than me, and I'd laughed at their lust for revenge. I just bought another round of drinks. By the end of the evening they were threatening to go around to my place and throw her out. I couldn't do that to her. No matter what, I'd loved her once. Perhaps...

I feel your passion in the question too. "Yes," I say. I feel nothing.

"What rules did she break, Claire?"

I melt again at my name tripping off your lips and have to work hard not to be consumed by the feeling burning at my crotch. I feel something now, I want to say. I smirk, and you study me quizzically. You're still waiting for a bloody rule. "Trust," I say.

You nod vigorously. "Good."

Great. I always trusted my ex would do what was right for her, so I'm not sweating that one. You're happy with my response, because your shoulders sit a little lower, your cheeks shine, and the lines that run along your forehead soften. You look pretty. "Do you want to go for a drink?" I ask. It hasn't occurred to me that you might refuse. Your lips tighten. I've missed the mark.

"I can't do that, Claire."

The rejection is an assault, a sharp, tearing blow to my chest. I savour the novelty of the unfamiliar feeling. *Wow.* "Okay," I say.

I'm fine. I feel nothing again. As I leave your office though, I know you're the one for me. You and me are soul mates. You're the one I've been waiting for all my life. I've known you a nanosecond, and in that short time felt rejection, attraction, lust, and a connection deeper than the deepest ocean. It's so fucking corny, but I think you have too, though I hope you didn't feel rejected. Seems like you've had enough of that for a lifetime. My heart aches as I walk from your office to my flat. It's a short distance, yet I feel light years away from you. The days before my next appointment drag like those last moments before the war has ceased. Danger lingers in the uncertainty. Who has been informed? Who is still fighting?

4.

When I see you again I sense you're a little more guarded. It's as though you've talked to yourself, rationalised your emotions, and come out on the other side. Your fingers touch mine as you hand me the clear plastic cup of water. It's a strange sensation, not as tender as I'd imagined it would be every day this previous week. You're stronger than you realise. You need to be, to hide your emotions, I think. They're strong in you, aren't they? We are opposites in that way.

You move behind the desk with exaggerated efficiency, clear your throat, pick up your pen, write something on the paper. When you look at me it's from a distance. I get it. You're protecting yourself like the boys I briefed before going to Afghan. They were trying to be brave, but the novelty and excitement had transmuted long before their trucks dived into the bowels of the ship that would carry them to their destiny. Some never returned. Fear is *your* guide.

"How have you been?" you ask.

I shrug. I've come to realise I do that a lot. It means I don't really know the answer to the question. I don't think I'm deliberately hiding something but you think I am, because you purse your lips while waiting for me to give you something you can get your mind around. "Sad," I say. That's the truth.

Your eyebrows lift. You weren't expecting that from me.

"Sad?"

You repeat the word in a questioning tone. It's what all good therapists do.

"You triggered something, last time we met."

Your shoulders drop, your guard plummets, and when you hold my gaze I see into your soul. I know it. You know it. Anyone looking at us both would know it. Right at that most precious moment, I see you and you see me. I'm not looking away as I'm processing you. You can't avoid me either. You have so much sadness. I've felt it drowning me in waves since I left your office the previous week. Since you stepped into the room to deliver that training, I've known your pain and suffering in the burning in my heart, the tension in my gut. Much use those techniques have been, eh? They can't touch empathy of this profundity. Who do you talk to, I wonder? You do that swallowing thing again, and your right eye twitches. I read this as a signal that I've touched a nerve.

You bring your hand to your mouth, then revert to the comfort of the pen in your hand, and scribble on the paper. I watch your energy withdraw as if it were a physical reality. It is. Your skin becomes tighter, your features sharper, your smile disappears, and your mind dominates the room.

"Triggered you how?"

"How?" I look to the window in reflection. I don't know how to answer. I know *what* you triggered, but I haven't got a clue *how*? Dumb question. It's only later that I come to realise the *how*. You stole my heart, that's *how*. You stepped inside me and stole my fucking heart. You haven't yet told me you're with someone, but why would you? It's none of my business whether you have a lover, a girlfriend, or a husband. In that exquisite moment, none of that matters. My business is your business. Your business is none of mine. Those are the rules, right? I don't get those rules. There's more to us already, you know. It's me and you. The physical space between us doesn't exist. We are one, united by something intangible. You feel it too.

"How were you triggered, Claire?"

You address my blank mind again, and a flood of sadness flows into me. Tears sit on the verge of exposure. I talk to them. I don't want you to see me this way. I can't explain the reason for the feeling, but you'll want me to try. If my throat constricts any further I swear it'll break my neck. The burning starts there, builds, becomes excruciating, then I swallow, and it recedes slowly. I am minded of the process of orgasm. The build-up is agonising, the release exquisite. "Your sadness triggered me," I say, though I don't recognise my voice, and then I watch you intently.

You slide your tongue repeatedly across your lower lip, bite at the inside of your upper lip, and your eyes refuse to settle. Emotional confusion challenges your intellect, and I feel my heart melt at the pain you hide so well—from others. You can't hide from me.

You gather yourself, present a tight-lipped smile, your gaze vacant.

"Tell me about *your* sadness, Claire?"

I fill my lungs slowly. I'm pondering me. I felt a bit sad after my mum died. Shocked. And I cried once, because suddenly she wasn't here anymore. The sadness lifted quickly though. I felt sad when my best mate got blown to bits in Iraq, but that too was a moment in time. I didn't feel sad when my client was killed. Pissed, yes. We'd failed him. I run these events through my mind now, and there's still nothing. No sadness. I'm resigned to reality, I guess. It's like they never really left me. I just can't see them anymore. I can't visit, share a drink, laugh, cheek, or banter with them. I hold them closer in my heart than I ever did in any hug that we shared. I think I'm different from other people. I know others feel sadness for years after a bereavement. I don't understand how they do that anymore than they can appreciate that I don't. You might be more like them than me on this front. Loss is an inevitable part of life. Maybe, I've just never loved enough. That allegation has often been levied at me. Maybe they've all been right. "I don't feel sad," I say. I'm confused.

Your lips twitch upwards just a fraction, barely perceptible. "You just said you were triggered with sadness."

You're hovering the pen over the paper. You're right, and I nod, but I can't explain it. I shrug, look to the window. When I turn back I stare into your eyes. You're combative in your unwavering gaze. I like that. I can't bluff you. I don't want to. That's not why I'm seeing you. I feel something when I'm with you, you see. I have since I first set eyes on you. Then it dawns to me. "I guess the sadness comes in knowing my heart can't have what it wants," I say.

I can't say that my heart wants you, though I'm optimistic things will change between us. I've seen you, haven't I? You hold my gaze a little longer, processing my words. Are you questioning my sincerity, or are you relating to what you might regard as true? I'm wondering how long you can resist admitting you want me too? "Do you think love and sadness are inextricably linked?" I ask. I'm genuinely interested in your thoughts on the topic.

You break eye contact. You're not used to a client asking you questions of a theoretical or conceptual nature.

I heard them all at the training day. They wanted to know how to solve their problems, how to rid themselves of negativity. They wanted to transform their lives by removing or denying aspects of themselves. I've always figured negativity exists because positivity exists. It's just a feeling riding the waves of our thoughts. The duality at play. You can't have one without the other. It's always intrigued me, why people are so quick to want rid of feelings they're uncomfortable with. Discomfort keeps us awake at night, it keeps us alive, has us fighting for our lives. Do they not know that every emotion passes in time? It's just energetic feedback. But even fear has an end to it, and it comes more quickly if you let it run its course.

Ride the waves, my friends, I wanted to tell them, but they wouldn't get it. And I couldn't be bothered to enter into debate with them. They wouldn't spar with me anyway, just look at me through confusion and think of me as a weirdo. I would've made matters worse for them, raised stuff they couldn't handle. It was your show, not mine. You're still thinking, aren't you?

And then you look into my eyes.

"I think loss has a big part to play in our sadness," you say softly, blinking as you say the words. "Love is pure. Love isn't sadness, but the loss of love can lead us to feeling sad."

I nod. "I get that. But love exists beyond loss too, doesn't it? Do you think you can feel loss without sadness? Does the absence of something or someone necessarily lead to the feeling of sadness? Or is sadness related to us wanting and not being able to have? Isn't sadness more closely linked to us not getting what we want?"

I'm relentless, I know. My passion comes through in this way, and it always has. I'm excited to find someone I can talk to about this stuff. I'm not an academic, just an average Jo with a fascination for the deeper side of our existence. We are complex, beautiful in our imperfections, striving to survive in a cruel world in which we feel inadequate and unappreciated. Or maybe, that's just me. My life. My world. I stare out the window, pondering whether you'll give my questions due consideration.

"I don't know," you say in almost a whisper.

I'm not disappointed. Who does know? At least we're talking as equals. I'm not your client when we talk like this. You're studying me, your eyes narrowing with your assessment. Something has shifted in you, I think. I sense you want to talk in more detail, but this is neither the time nor the place.

It takes another three sessions before you ask me the question I think was burning your lips at that time.

"What do you want that you can't have, Claire?"

Heat engulfs me. My name on your lips has never felt so good. I stare into your eyes, the desk fading between us, and I know you're expecting my response. "You," I say.

The thrill hits you almost imperceptibly but enough to confirm my suspicions. You *wanted* me to say those words.

5.

You speak to your supervisor about me. You must. She will stop you from moving to the next name on the list in your hand, because she senses something in the tone of your voice when you mention my name. Can she read you as well as I can?

"Justine, tell me more about your work with Claire," she will say to you.

You'll look at the notes on your pad and realise how sparse they are, see the doodles that have grown larger on the page with each session. That's how you distract your mind from that which you don't want to acknowledge. You won't be studying your notes. You'll be too consumed by the feelings that have haunted you since you started working with me, even before then if you dared admit it to yourself. I've triggered something in you too, haven't I?

"She's emotionally detached. Intelligent. PTSD is indicated given her history," you'll say, because that's what you see through the lens of your own past.

She will study you closely, spot your weakness. She will want me off your books, for your own protection, and ask you, "Can we sign off her fitness to work assessment?"

You'll feel the statement as a winded blow to the chest. You'll be compelled to trace the last sentence you wrote, *I want you.* You'll imagine caressing my body, your fingers ablaze with sensation, your soft gaze reflecting your desires.

You won't be in control of the short breath that escapes before you answer her question.

You will say, "I wouldn't be confident yet. She talked about her ex. There's bound to be trauma from the military and grief from the recent loss of her mother and client, though there are no explicit signs of avoidance or anxiety. No indication of guilt or shame. No overestimation of control or self-blame."

Nothing stacks up, does it, Justine? That knowledge will cause you to pause before you summarise the key points.

"She seems well adjusted. I don't get any indication of affective disorder."

But you'll still be mystified by the sadness. You self-medicate to cope with it, don't you, Justine? I've been bemused by your sadness too, since I first set eyes on you.

Your words will escape you in a whisper through thinned lips that deflect from your own secrets.

"She has experienced sadness in the last week," you will say.

You won't tell her that it was your sadness. How could you?

"She talks as if everything is matter-of-fact," you will say.

That's true.

"She was highly trained to cope with stress," she will tell you.

That's blindingly obvious. She's read the notes on my file. *Anyone* could tell you that.

"I agree."

I *am* highly trained. Special forces trained, in fact. I remember one of the officers interviewing me at the Career's office in my local town. He said that I might need to pick dead bodies off the street, and how did I feel about that? I had shrugged. The notion didn't mean anything to me. I guess that's what made me good soldier material. Obedient, fearless. Classically ripe for military conditioning.

I guess the indoctrination started long before I joined the military. Maybe that's what drew me to an army career. I'd been bought up with a strong sense of discipline, drilled into me by my father. The cane would sit in the corner of the hallway by the front door. The metal buckle on his belt was the most punishing though. He would appear from the living room, the television blaring, his eyes glassy and gaze vacant. It was the authority in the sway in his posture that gave away what was coming next. We learn behaviours through repeated patterns, you see, not from the time of day or whether the sun is shining or rain is falling. The vacant gaze, the staggering movements, the hand reaching for the belt unhooking the buckle sliding the leather through the belt loops around his waist. I know what's coming long before the metal rips my skin. I learned that running doesn't help; I'll get caught eventually, and the pain of trying to escape will be far more severe. I learned quickly. The first sting is the hardest to take. After the third strike, you drift. Numbness is your saviour. It's amazing the instinct to protect one's head, cover your ears, block out the sound of your own screaming. That soft fleshy part of your body still feels every bite but your brain refuses to register it. You don't know this about me though. That's not your fault, Justine. I haven't told you, because I don't know how to have that conversation. I've never told anyone about my past. It would reveal too much about me, and worst still, it would encourage pity. The military, the war, my mum's death, my girlfriend's rejection: they're nothing in comparison to my experience of him.

"Is there any indication of self-medication?" she will ask you.

The go-to response. Everyone thinks of alcohol and drugs as the natural coping strategies for stress, especially in jobs like mine. She was trying to help you with your assessment. She couldn't know that I'm not like that. Does she know your drug of choice?

"Alcohol, daily. Nothing excessive though," you'll say.

I was honest with you about that. I'm not a big drinker and I've never done drugs...well, a little weed back in the day. It's what we all did. You related when I told you, didn't you? I saw it in your rapidly blinking eyes, the personal reflection on darting memories. You gazed at the movement of my lips. I noticed you staring at me before you realised you were. Did you have a vision of me smoking, chilled, or was it something else that startled you? Do you recognise *your* life in the questions you have to ask me? Self-medication can be so subtle, can't it? Who doesn't have a glass of wine or two to unwind, eh? At what point does self-medication become destructive, I wonder.

And then she will ask you the question you didn't ask me, because it needs answering.

"Is there any sexual deviance?"

Your heart will race at the thought and words will evade you. Your hesitation will be noticed as you hide behind the reading of your notes and the patterned doodles. Blinded, consumed by your vivid, colourful imagination, you will stutter, because you haven't asked about my sexual pleasures.

Why *hadn't* you asked, Justine? You didn't strike me as the sexually deviant kind, I have to say. Did you think I might be? That idea amuses me.

Your supervisor will look at you over the top of her glasses and lean forward, assessing you quizzically. Your inner child will rise up at the perceived threat, and you'll feel it in the heavy pounding of your heart. I can't help but wonder if you'll sit shaking your head from side to side in small movements as you swallow, trying to comprehend your ineffectiveness, just as I've seen you do in our sessions.

You will say, "I don't know, but I didn't get that impression."

Then you'll take a deep sigh. It will be one of the first questions you ask me at our next session. Do you want to know? I think you do... Desperately.

"She keeps her cards close to her chest," you will say, defensive.

You're right.

"Protection?"

Your supervisor really is trying to help you.

"She strikes me as a private individual, self-reliant," you will say. "She comes across as grounded, smart. Emotionally guarded, yes, but who isn't?"

You know guarded well, don't you?

You'll shrug, I'm sure of that. Your supervisor will look at you with empathy. She's been in this position before. She knows how strong the pull is. That's why she can see the danger signs long before you will acknowledge them.

Not that there's a problem with me that you haven't detected. I'm not concealing something from you that you should have uncovered. The danger is far bigger than any threat I could pose. You. You're unable to maintain the professional boundaries between us. And we've already crossed the line, haven't we? She will easily sense your struggle. I did.

"Are you okay with this case?"

You'll nod, though uncertainty will parch your mouth. And, when you eventually say, "Yes," the timbre of your voice will expose you. You'll fight not to let flaming heat colour your cheeks. You might even think you've won the battle with her, with me. You'll trick yourself into thinking that you've gripped your emotions, refocused your mind, and taken back control.

The next time we meet you're flummoxed, because it isn't during a scheduled appointment, and you're caught unprepared.

6.

I notice you at the counter before you realise I'm there. My heart reminds me I'm still alive with a firm rhythmical beat. My pulse quickens with the imprint of you on me. You're looking up at the menu of drinks as if considering the multitude options. The reddish tints in your fair hair have come to life under the spot lighting, liberated, freed from the constraints of the band you tie it back with when you're at the office. You should wear it down more often. My imagination is already at the point of running my fingers through the long waves, tugging your body close to mine, enjoying the shudder of pleasure that zips through me.

I watch you talking to the barista. She knows you, because this is your regular haunt. The coffee is good. You order the caramel cortado. That too, I discover, is your regular drink. It's not about the coffee though, is it? You don't care for the difference in taste between a latte or an Americano. It's about time. There will never enough of it for you. Speed may provide the illusion of self-importance, but it also means you're too busy to address the pain that haunts you and causes you to rush through your life. You try to give the impression you're making a choice when you're just playing the same old cards you know so well. Security is important to you, isn't it? All that time spent studying the options...did you really think you'd take a chance on anything else? I'm disappointed. The cortado is a short coffee which means you won't be hanging around for long. You hand over the loyalty card and some cash, then take your change, move to the side of the counter, and await your drink. That's when you notice me in the line, two customers back from being served.

You have the look of a naughty child having just been spotted by their parent before you gather your thoughts. Your soft smile is slow to form but when it comes, it's warm. Your eyes are so beautiful I could lose myself in them. You acknowledge me with the slightest nod of your head. I order my drink as yours is handed to you.

"Hello, Claire. How are you?"

You sound too formal.

"I'm okay." Okay is my stock response. I'm *okay* all the time. Your right eye does that twitching thing, and your lips part slightly. You want to talk to me, but the boundaries forbid it, right?

"Can I sit with you?" I ask, before you can put up any barriers. Your lips close, the resignation within your deep breath is clear to me.

"Yes, of course," you say.

You head for a table, knowing I'm watching your back and the sensual sway of your hips as you walk. When you turn and sit, you look radiant. Colour darkens your skin, softens your features. I see you. Not the therapist, not the trainer. You.

I knew by the time I got to the table you would've finished your coffee so I place another in front of you. "I took the liberty," I say and shrug.

Your cheeks are still glowing. Your smile conveys genuine gratitude. The lines that seemed ever present in our therapy sessions are absent. You look younger, more casual.

"Thank you. You didn't need to do that," you say.

I make a movement with my head that's a kind of nod, tilt, and shrug all at the same time to say that it's no problem. Sitting opposite you, I sip at my extra-hot latte in a tall glass. It burns my tongue, the way I like it. "Do you have a day off?" I ask. You sip the cortado with your head down before briefly glancing up at me.

"Yes."

It's going to be a warm autumn day according to the forecast. The parks in London are glorious this time of year. I'm feeling brave. No, I want to spend time with you, get to know you. That's what drives me to ask you.

"Would you like to go for a walk? It's going to be a beautiful day."

You would not believe how hard my heart is pumping right now. It's like the feeling you get knowing you're being watched, expecting something bad to happen and hoping for something amazing. Adrenaline. I fucking love that drug. Your eyes study everyone in the café, avoiding me while the justifications for and against the proposition play out in your mind. You know you shouldn't entertain the idea of spending social time with a client, but you feel *it* too. We're polar opposites drawn with a force so powerful there isn't anything that can stop the imminent collision. You know it. I know it. Who cares what others think? That's always been my motto. I wouldn't hurt anyone, but my business is my business. I'm not one for following social norms, and I don't think you are either. Whatever. At this moment the energy between us is stronger than your need for social approval. Right now, you're the blinkered horse in a one-horse race. You have no choice but to follow the track your feelings are dictating. Actually, it's how you always roll.

You nod. "I have an hour," you say.

I've never felt more alive. I refrain from grinning broadly, but the way you're holding my gaze tells me you can see how good I feel. I'm beaming inside, warm and fuzzy, and brimming with optimism. I expect you'll ask questions as we walk. I'm okay with that. Today you are not my therapist.

I hadn't expected the awkwardness between us. Do you feel it? The push and pull, of willpower versus desire. We have a similar stride length. It's unusual to find a woman who effortlessly matches a military pace. We walk in step, in tune. My hands are firmly rammed inside my jean pockets while yours hang freely at your side.

"Have you been a therapist long?" I ask, hoping to ease the tension.

"I qualified three years ago."

You're watching the ground at your feet, and your pace has shortened. Now we're ambling. It's nice. "Do you enjoy your work?"

"Yes. It's challenging. And rewarding. It's testing me."

Your tone shifts to thoughtful. I can't help but think you're referring to working with me. You glance at me then back to the ground.

"What about you? Do you enjoy your work?" you ask.

I shrug. "I get a kick out of knowing I'm protecting people." It's how I feel. You look at me with an intense frown then stop walking and stare out at the rippled water that flows beneath the footbridge.

"Would you really give your life for someone you barely know?" you ask.

I hear a hint of scepticism in your voice. I see disbelief in the narrowing of your gaze, and it makes me smile. "Yes."

You blink at the conviction in my tone, look to the water, perhaps giving your attention to your thoughts.

I want you to look at *me*. *I* want your attention. I need you to see *me*. "I never think about death when I'm with a client. I never dwelt on the possibility of dying in an act of duty when I was serving either. I know it could happen, but there's just no point in thinking about it. If I did mull the possibilities, I'd be less effective and cause problems. You can't think about it, and if something kicks off, there's simply no time to think at all. You become consumed with the execution of the plan." I'm trying to explain to help you understand me. My brain works differently from others, you see. You're nodding, but I can tell you don't get it. I find that truth about you endearing. "You help people in a different way, and that's cool," I say.

"I try to."

You huff, look over my shoulder and into the distance, and sigh.

I'm left thinking you don't believe in yourself. "Surely all you can do is try. It's down to the client what they do with the information you give them. You can't save anyone. No one can save another from the mental and emotional trauma that we experience during our lives. It's not like physically removing someone from harm. The internal stuff is different. We need to save ourselves, take responsibility for our thoughts, feelings, and behaviours. You show us how to claim our power back. You show us how to do that, Justine."

I love the feel of your name on my lips. I've been rehearsing it in the privacy of my flat. I'm trying to help you feel better about yourself and what you do. I know I haven't been an easy client to work with, but I don't want you thinking that's your fault. It isn't. I'm not broken. I have nothing for you to heal.

"That's true," you say.

Your smile conveys such profound sadness I feel it tug at my chest. The urge to hold and comfort you commands my feet, and before I know it I'm a pace closer to you. You don't move away. You stare vacantly at me. Where do you go to? There's darkness inside that mind of yours. Please let me in. Your mouth summons me. It reveals your heart's desire in the same way your eyes broadcast your pain and suffering. You are an enigma. A beautiful, enchanting enigma.

You seem to return to the moment, become aware that we're close to touching. Did my breath cause your skin to tingle? You turn your head from my gaze and look to the thousands of stars dancing on the surface of the water.

"It's beautiful, isn't it?" I ask. My tone is affected by the shift in proximity, the ache in my heart screams at me to hold you close. It takes all my conditioned restraint to not put my hand on the small of your back. I thrust tight fists into deep pockets that pull down on my hip. I rock my shoulders and shiver though I'm not cold. I couldn't explain to you what I'm feeling if you asked me now, therapist to client. It would be too hard to define. Love? How can it be love? We haven't long met. Protection? I know *that* feeling, and this is qualitatively different. Why is it so important to me that you're happy? I shouldn't care. I have no reason to care this deeply about you. But I do. I know you by heart.

"Were you brought up in London?" I ask. I haven't been able to place you. Your skin is fair, your hair dark, and your accent comes from nowhere in particular.

"No," you say.

I wait to see if you're going to offer any more. But you stay silent for some time, your chest moving rhythmically, and your eyes firmly set on the water.

My heart is aching, sensing that you're close to tears. You try to look casual, rub at your eyes with an indignant flick. Then you turn sharply towards me. Have you lost all sense of spatial awareness? Did you stumble, or did you mean to move closer?

Your breath, the heat from your body, the fire in your eyes. I know what's coming next and so do you. My thoughts silence the instant your mouth comes to mine. My senses become lost in the tenderness of pliant wet lips barely touching mine, firm breasts hot to mine, the strength of your arm, your hand squeezing my waist. You're trembling, and so am I. Your hair falls like silk through my fingers. I've dreamed of this. I knew it was you. So soft. So tender. Unhurried, languid, sensing, we become lost in a moment that can never be repeated. The first kiss. Longing, desire, lust, blossoming, and so full of expectation. For what feels like an eternity we dance together in blissful union. If your supervisor was to walk this way, what would she think? The thought passes in a flicker, the taste, the texture of you quieting my mind. I feel you. You feel me. We have no need to breathe almost, no desire for anything more than this moment can provide. It's exquisite, and we know there's no going back. The truth cannot be denied. When we ease out of the embrace, the darkness has lifted from your eyes, and your smile is lighter. My heart is soft, exposed. Then you look up in a moment of abject realisation, and the darkness descends.

"You're not my therapist," I whisper.

You shake your head. I cup your cheek. You can't look at me. I want you to look at me like you did just a second ago. You don't, and I'm confused. "You're not my therapist, Justine," I say again, trying to catch your evasive eyes. You shake your head again, look up to avoid the tears that pool in your eyes.

"It's not about you," you say.

I let you go and ram my hands into my pockets. I resist the shutters that are begging to close around my heart. I'm not done yet, and I don't think you are either. It's just fucking shit timing. You feel guilty, because you're a professional who has crossed boundaries. I wish you wouldn't. Please don't blame yourself.

I take a pace back, give you space. You look tense, worried, and there's darkness in your eyes that runs so deep. "I'm sorry," I whisper. What I mean is, I'm sorry we're not free to go where our hearts want us to be. You're biting your top lip. Are you angry with yourself? "It's not your fault, Justine."

You shake your head, evasive, refusing to look at me for more than a fleeting glance as you shift attention from the park over my left shoulder to the water over my right.

"I need to go," you say.

You turn and walk away, leave me standing gazing at your back as you head towards the exit.

The shivering happens of its own volition, stemming from the seed you just sowed. The feeling seeks refuge in the rash that prickles my skin. I wrap my arms around my chest, my teeth begin to chatter. What just happened? What will happen next between us? I lean out over the bridge, absorb myself in the river flowing below my feet. The water that bashes against the unyielding stone, I relate to that. It's like our resistance to the flow of emotion. You have the power to break my heart. I know that now. Don't ask me how it happened, because I wouldn't be able to tell you. I've never felt this way before. I'm not afraid to admit the meaning of it scares the shit out of me.

I see your reflection in the ripple of the stream, the sadness that fills you in the setting of the sun. The taste of you that lingers on my dry lips. I fear if I move from this spot on the bridge I will lose it all, but it's getting darker and colder, and I need to head home. I don't recall how many times I've looked around the park in the last hours hoping to see you striding towards me. I glance around one last time. I don't see you. I didn't expect to really.

Retracing our steps, I find myself at the café counter ordering a caramel cortado. Our table is occupied. A woman reading a book is sat in your seat facing into the room, mine opposite her is empty. I sit at the table next to her, face the wall, and imagine you're there talking to me about where we might go for supper later. It's not glamourous, I know, but it's the sort of thing couples do, right?

I must have said something, because the woman looks up from her book, gazes at me sternly then moves an inch further from me even though I'm nowhere near her. Nutter! I can't help but chuckle, and you giggle too. We're naughty kids having fun at no one's expense. I love the way you smile when you're this happy.

7.

I anticipated the call from your office asking me if I would be willing to move to another therapist. Still, my heart drops into a deep, dark well of disappointment, so, so claustrophobic in that place. If I wasn't well trained I would have a panic attack. Instead, I simply decline their kind request. The line is silent for some time. The music is relaxing though. Baroque, right? I've always liked Vivaldi so I'm happy to wait. Does the receptionist speak to you before acceding to you honouring our next session? Do you have to clear it with your supervisor? I doubt you did, even though you probably should. The woman seems hesitant when she confirms our appointment. I'm sensitive to her discomfort and thank her profusely.

Putting the phone down, thoughts of seeing you flood me with a reassuring glow of anticipation. It hasn't occurred to me that you might be suffering. In retrospect it's selfish of me to insist on seeing you, but I don't have the strength, the will, or the desire to do anything differently. My attraction to you is as the sun's relationship is to the earth. Nothing stops it emerging. Nothing gets in its way. Yes, clouds come but clouds go. Not being able to see you this week is the thunderstorm threatening overhead, obscuring the warmth of the sun. It's going to be a very long week.

When I enter the building and step into the lift, my hands are clammy. My hands are never clammy. I rub them vigorously down the coarse material of my jeans until my palms sting and radiate dry heat. As I approach the low reception desk and look down at the seated clerk, my heart pounds to escape my chest. The urge to run is powerful at times like those. Not that there is anything real to fear in this moment, except a broken heart I guess. And then, you appear in the reception area before I take my seat, and for the first time in my life, I freeze. Thought evades my brain. Movement challenges my muscles. My mouth is as parched as Death Valley in the Mojave Desert. Do you know that the temperature there reached a hundred and thirty-four degrees once? Swallowing is like trying to throw a bag of nails down my throat, until the water softens the cracked, crinkled flesh. You hand me a glass of water as if you sensed my struggle.

"Come in, Claire."

Your tone is unmistakably professional, your smile acquiescent to our plight as you move to your desk. That there is no doubting in my mind what is coming next doesn't help the words land any softer. You can't hold my gaze.

"Claire, we need to talk about what happened the other day."

At least you're brave enough to acknowledge something happened. I'm not looking for an apology then and don't know that wasn't your style anyway. The water tastes good. I control my pulse, a strong, steady beat, and watch you for the signs I've already come to know. You lift your head, keep your eyes down, scribble something on the pad, then lift your chin and look directly at me.

"We can't see each other again, Claire."

My pulse thunders until I challenge it with my interpretation of your desires. You don't mean it, I tell myself. Your eye twitches, you wet your lips, and clear your throat. I want to ask you, why not? But, I know the answer so what's the point?

I stare at you. "What do you need to know to get me cleared for work?"

You look to your notes, perhaps they're the ones from the session with your supervisor.

"What strategies do you use to deal with stress, Claire?" you ask.

I must be frowning, because you repeat the question and ask how I cope? Do I exercise? Do I meditate? You still don't ask me about sex. If you do, I'll tell you that I can take it or leave it.

"I run, cycle, swim, go to the gym. There isn't a day in the week when I don't work out. It's a habit I created in the military, one that's hard to put down. I enjoy being fit. It means I can eat what I want, when I want. I don't fuss about dieting and all that shit that seems to occupy copious hours of people's lives. My ex was one of those, always checking the contents of the packet before deciding whether to live or not."

You nod, make a note. "Meditation?" you ask.

"I did a retreat once. Silence is my friend. I can be content alone with my thoughts and lonely in the company of people."

You stare at me as if I'm talking in alien speak. That makes me soften inside, and I smile. And for a moment I see a glimmer of recognition in your eyes. It's nothing to do with what I've just said but everything to do with what you and I share. It's not quite a foot in the door, not even a wedge, but it's a start. It gives me hope. Do I amuse you, Claire?

I want to take our session seriously, convince you to see me again. I stare at the hands in my lap like they belong to someone else. My mind drifts. "It takes at least twenty years to perfect the art of meditation." I learned that when I took leave in Goa. My ex wasn't into yoga. She thought I was fucking nuts.

I look up to find you staring at me, eyes filled with expectation yet empty through disconnection. How do you do that? Where is your heart? Do you even feel your heart beating? Sorry, I'm distracted by you. My tone sounds weary as I continue with the story. "I went with a colleague, an officer."

You pinch your lips and swallow, as if preparing to speak.

"No, we weren't having an affair." You smile because I do. "We were good friends, though we shouldn't have been given the rank difference between us. We were kindred spirits. India is a beautiful part of the world. Have you been?"

You shake your head.

"We spent two weeks in Goa, Mandrem Beach. Longer would have been better but leave was restricted. The place was set in a palm grove. We sat for hours in the shade of the tall palm-trees, doing nothing, being nothing. Do you know

49

how many thoughts pass through our mind in just a few seconds?" I pause, testing my mental strength. Thoughts drift into my awareness. I watch them then let them free. And then the sense of your soft lips delicately pressed to mine comes to me, and my mind locks onto the image with the tenacity of a starving tiger trapping its prey. I can't shake it off. Not because I'm not trained to, but because I don't want to let it go. I feel the effect of it burning between my legs. The intensity has blindsided me, and I'm staring at you, craving you.

I think you thought the same thing because your eye twitches. I can't dwell on my wants though, or you'll get scared off again. You clear your throat. You still have that stern look in your eyes.

"Do you still meditate?"

I nod. "Not as often as I did." I need to tell the truth. I look out the window. "I'm not sure why I stopped the regular practice. At my peak I was getting up at four a.m. to meditate for an hour and then for another hour last thing in the evening. I was in a really good place then. It's hard to explain the feeling to someone who hasn't meditated. It's like you live in a completely different world. Time doesn't exist. It's just space. You're observing everything. Stress doesn't exist either, at least not as a lingering, niggling, parasitic response as most people experience it. Yes, you feel it in the moment you're under threat. We're human after all. But it's a point in time."

You're frowning at me as I ramble, but the lines between your eyes are softer than they were. I want to help you to understand me. "Meditation isn't a cocoon. It's not a delusional place where nothing bad ever happens."

I scratch my head. I always scratch my head when trying to find the right words to explain things. I'm not bright enough, you see. I don't have an extensive vocabulary, and words can be inadequate descriptors of our experience. Do you pick up that scratching is a small sign of my frustration with myself? It's a minor point and nothing to make a case with, but you need to see me. Not being able to describe something doesn't mean I don't feel stuff. My senses have always been true to me. They've never let me down. Think, damn it.

You smile, encouraging me without invading the space with impoverished words that would direct my reflections.

"It's the difference between feeling oppressed and free. The time immediately before an attack, before the first gunshot. The first assault is the worst. You feel the tiniest you have ever felt. The tightest knot you could ever tie grips your chest. The most important thing, the one thing that keeps you sane at that moment, keeps you from diving into a pit of despair that your life is going to end, is to control your thoughts. If you don't, that knot will strangle the life out of you before enemy fire has been launched. You'll become the insignificant being that you feel you are. That's the danger. Stress will get you killed in a nanosecond, as well as everyone around you. So, it's simple. No thought, no stress."

"You never feel stressed?"

You're not listening to me. You can't. I didn't know it then, but how could you appreciate what it's like to be free from stress when your world is suffocated by the very essence of it? I'm squinting at the pain of your incomprehension. Shit. I really need you to get this. I take in a deep breath, release it slowly. "Yes, I feel stress in the moment it's happening, but the feeling moves through me quickly. I guess my senses are alerted to the danger, then conditioning kicks in, and I give my attention to dealing with the situation, the enemy. Afterwards, what's the point in harping back? I've never seen the sense in regurgitating the last meal. Too much acid poisons our memories, right?"

You pull your lips into a thin line and although you're nodding, you don't think it's possible to let go of stress that easily, do you?

Believe me. It is. "Stress is a choice," I say.

Your eyebrows shoot up, and I want to laugh. You said the same thing to us in the training, so I'm not surprised by your reaction. Remember, I've endured many training sessions and motivational briefings over the years. What's said in the classroom often bears no relation to what's actually achievable. Maybe that's what makes me different to your other clients. You won't change jack shit sitting in a room being lectured to. You have to get off your arse and do something if you want your life to change.

"When were you last stressed?"

I hold your gaze wondering if you will look away, and if so at what point will your eyes divert to the comfort of the innocuous. The water cooler? The pad in front of you? The door, an escape route? Your top lip quivers. You don't like silence, do you? I'm not playing games with you. I won't subject you to the pain of your repetitive, tormenting thoughts. "I'm stressed now," I say and shrug. It's my stock response, did you know? I don't mean to be impudent, it's just a physical release for me.

It's the truth. It might not be an identical feeling to the pre-battle surge. It's subtle. A low hum, a soft tingling in the base of my ribs. It should be easy enough to handle, but it's like a damn light that won't go out. Burning there, a torturous torch igniting my heart, the threat of rejection flickering at its tip, keeping me alert to the risk of being here in close proximity to you.

You close your eyes which confuses me. Are you challenged by tears? You open your eyelids slowly though not fully and huff softly through your nose. Then you do that thing with your tongue rolling around your top teeth and wet your lips.

"Why are you stressed now?"

Your voice is groggy, weary even. The flickering flame of an impending rebuff begins to blister my skin. I'm resilient in battle though. I know I'm gasping for the cool air to slow my racing heart. My skin tingles from the burst of heat that swept through me. You cause this kind of stress. I look to the window, steady my lustrous thoughts. "I haven't felt like this before," I say.

You tilt your head. I've given you a problem to explore, haven't I?

"How is this stress different?"

I hold your gaze. "Because it won't go away."

You nod. "Do you want it to go away?"

Your head is still on a tilt. You look innocent. Cute. "No." My voice is alien to me.

The word is so short yet lingers excruciatingly in our mutual appreciation of each other's desires. I know this because your cheeks darken, and the knuckles on your hand become visible as you jot down a note.

You glance at the watch hanging loosely around your wrist. It's a fashion statement, isn't it? The Rolex. Do you like the way it clatters against the desk as you work? The rhythmical beat of it reminding you that you're doing well in your job, financially, I mean? You've become someone, haven't you? You put the pen down, clasp your hands together on the desk, and look at me. Please don't let that be pity in your eyes.

"I'm not sure how much I can help you, Claire."

I'm shaking my head long before you finish that sentence. I genuinely think we're getting somewhere.

"I'll sign off your fitness to work certificate and get a letter sent across to the agency later today."

You sound officious. It doesn't suit you. When you stand, I stand. You walk to the door, and I follow you. You make a mistake though. You don't open the door as I was expecting. You stop, turn, and face me, and I'm too close to you for comfort. Your body heat, the scent of you, it's too much. I can't ignore the effect of you on me. You've crushed every ounce of restraint I might have once had, and I don't care. But this isn't all about me, is it? Because, you, you stand so perfectly still, and your eyes provoke me to make the first move. You can't. Your moral compass tries to clip the wings of your desire. But your heart is screaming, crying, begging for me. You're trembling. I didn't mean to touch your breast. So soft, but your nipple, so rigid. The duality of your personality reflected in one body part, stripped bare. Tenderness and stubbornness. Which one will win when it comes to us, Justine? I know the answer to that question long before I kiss you again. I want to draw the tenderness from you, show you that it's okay to love with an open heart. There are no conflictual thoughts in the groan that escapes your lips. None. That, my love, was pure, guttural pleasure.

And you know it.

You don't pull away.

You don't stop kissing me.

You groan again as you explore my breast, as your thumb trips over the firmness you fashioned just by being you. I can be stubborn too.

Do you think you'll be able to concentrate on the young man I see sat on the couch in your room when I leave?

8.

I wait in the park on the old wooden bench in front of the ancient oak tree. There's a small bronze plaque in the centre of the backrest with an inscription as indistinguishable as the memory of the person's life it celebrated. It's a hunch on my part. Calculated, of course. I back my hunches, and I knew this one won't let me down. Coffee is bound to be on your agenda after meeting me. You will pass this bench to get from your office to your café of choice. I can still taste the caramel cortado. Can you still taste me on your lips, Justine?

Your pace slows as it catches up with your awareness of me smiling at you. I'd watched every step you'd taken with a racing heart. Knowing you were oblivious to my presence made the thrill electrifying. The weight of the day lifts from me as your stride increases once more.

Your body moves more freely when you relax, you know? Your shoulders sit like table tops still, but your arms have a playfulness about their movement, fitting for the animation you exude when you take the stage in your training room. I think you'd be very expressive if you allowed yourself the freedom to simply be you. Who knocked the innocence out of you, Justine? Was it your father? Just like me?

You don't smile when you see me, but you swagger in my direction. It's involuntary and slips through your control mechanisms. It's sassy, sexy, and I feel it in the feather-like sensation tickling low in my stomach and in the fire that challenges my ability to stand up straight.

"Claire."

"Justine." My tone is serious. I'm mocking impudence.

You smile, and there's a twinkle in your eyes.

You stare at me in an exasperated fashion, then look skyward, and out it comes. The joy of it speaks to my inner child who joined you. You are *so* beautiful when you laugh.

You gaze intently at me, eyes ablaze, stifle the bubble of delight that has taken you by surprise, then shake your head. I don't know what you're thinking. Whether you're cross with me or excited. Are you free to be with me? Have you reconciled your ethnical boundaries with your baser desire for me, with your absolute need for our connection? Are we really doing this? And what the fuck is this? So many questions numb my intuition. I'm thrown from the security of my own assurances, my faith in you. I close my eyes, slow down my racing thoughts, and refocus. I open them and see into you. You're looking at me. No longer the therapist guarded by the armour of title or rules. You. The about-to-be lover I've coveted for some time now. And me. In the openness between us in this moment, you let me inside.

"Do you want to go for a drink?" you ask.

The way you say it feels as though we have always been lovers.

The wine bar you lead me to is up-market with a large chandelier in the centre of the room above the circular bar. Soft, downlights cast a shadow of intimacy over the private booths around the room. It's not that I'm a spit-and-sawdust kinda girl, just middle-of-the-road. This is proper posh and shooting way above my pay packet. I'm usually the one stood close to the door of such places, monitoring the guests as they arrive, knowing my client is sampling the riches of life on the inside.

It's here I discover your penchant for fine wines, and your generosity when you insist on paying the exorbitant bill for our drinks.

You order a large glass of wine for you and a small one for me with a smile that would melt the most steel-hearted warrior. The bartender isn't all that, and she's easily seduced by your sensuality. I'm impressed. You have gravitas, and you're fucking hot.

More importantly you're here with me.

You lead me to an empty booth. We sit and gaze at each other in silence for the time it takes our drinks to arrive at the table. I'm comfortable with silence, but my insides are effervescent. You present that smile again and the barwoman looks like she's going to explode. I watch you watching her scuttle away. Are you really looking at her arse?

When you turn back to face me, look into *my* eyes, you seem deep in thought. You start talking without pause, and that's when you tell me about *her*, your girlfriend. As the words fall effortlessly from your lips, the sound becomes muffled to my ears. It's like a mortar going off close to my head: everything rings for a long time, then sounds and voices seem to expand and slow down at the same time. They're warped. In the aftermath of an explosion like that, words don't form coherently. Your mind is grappling to make sense of the assault, and then the hard, thundering beat of your heart reminds you that you're still alive. Wishes and desires are irrelevant to reality, aren't they? I cannot avoid the truth of your words, your life, and running from you won't serve me or us.

"What's she like?" I ask as I pick up the glass to take a sip. The sour taste seems all that more poignant for the conversation we are having.

"Kind. Loving."

I nod. I would expect no less. You wouldn't be with someone who wasn't kind and loving. My insides are turning over the disappointment. My mind is calm. It's well trained. There's something comforting about knowing, don't you think? Even if that which we find out we don't like to hear, there is at least certainty in the *knowing*. We can do something with certainty. Uncertainty, not knowing, that's our real enemy.

I try to hold your gaze as you tell me about her. But you're locked deep inside the world behind your eyes, the one in which your inner child sits alone, waiting to be rescued by the prince. It looks like a lonely place to me and makes you unreachable. I want to talk to you about the dark night of the soul that we all must pass through to evolve into better versions of ourselves, but it's too soon. The timing isn't right.

"She's a therapist," you say.

It's great you have a lot in common, I'm thinking. "That's nice," I say.

Military relationships always work better than mixed. I imagine it must be the same for mixed-race, mixed-anything really. There's so much more to overcome. Relationships are hard enough to navigate before you throw in differences of culture, belief structures, and value systems. It's a fucking nightmare in the making. You meet someone, you connect through commonality, you think you're like them. Boom! Big mistake. Only when you get into the relationship do these differences present themselves: in the subtle points of irritation, the distant tone in the argument, and then you stop talking altogether. Before that, it's all about the lust, the adoration, the sex, the thrill. I avoided all that. Not that you know anything about my past in this respect.

"I'm not in love with her."

Sometimes, a window opens when you're least expecting it. "What happened?"

You shrug, ponder the glass in your hand, and take a long swig but swallow in several small, steady gulps. You think you don't know the answer when really, you just can't face the truth. There's something lacking in her, isn't there? She can't sustain you, can she? We all get to that place, I think. We are all seekers, you see? We need others to fill the gaps in us that make us weak, vulnerable, susceptible to pain. We think we don't have what it takes to fill them ourselves. The lovers we take gratify our needs, until we wake up and realise they can't save us as we had expected. The gaps remain unfulfilled, grow wider with every passing year of our discontent. We're as inadequate as we ever were, and only then do we realise we can only save ourselves. It's a painful lesson and one we may not own until we've tried and failed with several relationships. We're the same, you and me. And yet, we are not.

"We grew apart, I guess. We want different things."

The sex is still good, you tell me. It's a measure of success for you, isn't it? You haven't suffered lesbian bed-death, you emphasise with a broad grin. And you've been with her since your last year at Oxford uni together, seven years, going on eight.

I wonder at the brain power in your house. It must make for interesting conversation over dinner of an evening. Must be nice to have someone to debate with. I didn't have that with my ex.

I wonder, briefly, at the age difference between us too. You'll know that from my case file. Do you find mature women attractive? "I don't subscribe to social bullshit when it comes to what's needed to make a relationship work," I say. You don't seem surprised at that.

"Me neither," you say.

And I believe you. "How often people have sex in a week, who gives a shit? Everyone's different in that respect. A relationship is always what it is: a work in progress, constantly developing, and evolving. There's no beginning and no end. We come together at a point in time designed by the actions of others before us. Maybe we continue into another dimension after this life. Who knows? What I do know is, but for a decision, that a meeting at a different time and place between our parents or our grandparents before them, you and I wouldn't exist in the same space. It's profound to think our start point was determined by the decisions of others. We could easily have never met. It's fate. A relationship is a journey we embark on together for as long as the road takes us in the same direction."

You're nodding, filtering my words through your psychologically trained perspective to find the points that match and the points of difference. I don't know what *you* really think, hell, neither do you, and it's much later in our relationship that I realise, deep down, we have very different perspectives on relationships.

You look at me, your thoughts revealed in sorrowful eyes that your heavy eyelids try to hide. It's not just about *her* though, is it?

You tell me you've cheated on her before now. Illicit affairs are a thrill. They ignite your passion and provide the illusion of freedom you so desperately crave, don't they? I can relate to the rush, the exhilaration. The feeling of liberation is so alluring.

Relationships in the military were undertaken underground, my love. This is my territory you're in now. I'm well trained in the art of secret seduction. The subtle glances across a crowded bar that you think no one else has noticed except her. You stand closer to her than the others, nod furiously as she talks into your ear as if in casual conversation for the world to see, while her hot breath against your skin turns your insides wild with desire. You will deny her to everyone, because you must. Your heart will ache for her in the darkness of night. You will risk being caught for the thrill. Silent sex is so mind-blowingly fucking hot, you come too quickly. She has to make sure the coast is clear before you leave her room. Being spotted will cost you everything. It's hard-arsed, and you love it. The difference is, that was the norm for us. It wasn't an affair. It was the mission, the love story played out in forbidden territory. High risk, high reward.

That's where we're at now, isn't it? The illicit affair about to begin. I'm not sure how I feel about being in an affair. "Are you going to tell her about us?" I hold your gaze, watch your mouth twitch.

"It's tough," you say and grab the passing waiter to order more drinks for us.

You tell me how much she needs you, how interdependent your lives have become over the years. You have a home together, two dogs, a cat called Tizzy, and a large tank of salt-water fish. They all have names too. I'm thankful you spare me the detail. You studied together at Oxford. You now work in the same building, take lunch at the same café, attend the same seminars. You have the same supervisor too.

I feel claustrophobic inside your world. There is escape in the ability to deny your relationship. The choice to withdraw into isolation is made easy by the constraints of military rules. No excuses are needed, you're just not going to take the risk anymore. No one challenges you. It's a way to remain safe, detached. Protect your interests and keep your heart intact. The physical release is there for you should the need arise, it always is, but even that loses its appeal over time. Sex for sex's sake lacks connection. Flirting on the other hand allows you to feel, and it's harmless, you tell yourself. There is no evidence of sexual impropriety in flirting. No one can prove a look means anything. Yet you get high on seducing her with your eyes then relieve yourself in the privacy of your room. Your body learns to experience physical gratification through a glance. Your imagination fills the gaps, and it is sublime.

What you forget is *they* don't need hard evidence to dismiss you from the service. Suspicion will suffice. The wrong artists in your record collection. The note you wrote many years earlier that she forgot to burn, filed inside the book with the wrong title. They look for the obvious, and you're guilty by association. Your life is nothing like mine was. You get high on your secret liaisons, the idea of having an affair, of doing something that might get you caught. It's the thrill, the fire that ignites your blood and reminds you that you're alive. Is it the attention you crave or the feeling of power? My secret liaisons were nothing like yours. No one got hurt. We all knew the rules. You're making a choice that will destroy someone.

"Why did you cheat on her?"

The waiter approaches, and you're grateful for time to consider the question. She smiles at you, but you don't see her.

"I don't know," you say.

Where does that mind of yours go to? I don't push you. You're hiding, and I've learned that people in hiding get *very* defensive *very* quickly when pushed to reveal their insights. Force serves no one. If you want me to know, you'll tell me. I respect that fact, though I can't help searching those eyes of yours. Again, you don't see me. You're busy, working with your thoughts, compartmentalising them, justifying your behaviours, and burying the feelings. Guilt still colours your skin, and your gaze leaps from me to scan the clientele around the room. Are you worried about us being seen together now? Does it dawn on you that I'm one of the people you will later deny to *her*? I can't imagine the pain and confusion, the complexity that forms your inner world. What are you really hiding from, my love? What truth is so hard for you to face?

Why am I finding it impossible to step away from you? Now would be a good time to do that, surely? But there are no alarm bells ringing in my ears. Compassion softens my aching heart. I see you. I feel your pulse in sync with mine, and your soul walking alongside mine. I know you are seeking a feeling. Who isn't? I recognise your pain as you look around the room. I don't think you're deliberately avoiding me. You're looking for something to hang your attention on. Distraction is your guide. I smile and ask you if you'd like to leave.

You nod and finish your drink. I leave mine.

Darkness has descended, and the air is fresh. It cuts through the tension between us, and you wrap your arm through mine as we walk. The physical contact surprises me. You are an enigma. You lean into me. You have the warmth of a glove caressing and soothing the hand inside. Tonight, my time with you is limited, and the station appears long before I'm ready to let you go. We stand outside, staring at each other. My hands are fisted, pressed deeply into my jean pockets. You want to kiss me. I want to kiss you. The risk is too great. I understand these rules. You're not familiar with exercising restraint though, are you? You've taken what you've wanted before and worried about the consequences later. I won't go there with you, not tonight.

You bite your lip. When you look at me your eyes are searching, hopeful.

"Will you spend a day with me?" you ask.

I can't resist another opportunity to see you, to talk with you. "When?"

"This Friday?"

I assume your partner must be away and nod.

Your smile lights up your face, softens your gaze, and draws me into your world. It takes every ounce of discipline I possess to not pull you into my arms and kiss you with lingering tenderness. I know if I did, I would do something I might regret. I would take you somewhere, anywhere, and fuck you until the morning light brings us to our senses.

We both want that, and more, I know. But I can't do that to her, and neither will you. Not this time.

I'm not the affair, am I?

This is different.

I am the lover who will later become your wife.

9.

Friday is a glorious autumn day. My favourite time of year. Shades of blue infuse a cloudless sky, the air is cool, and the sun is holding its warmth before conceding to the imminent winter greys that constitute our winter. I'm ten minutes early for our rendezvous on the corner of the road, about two hundred yards from my flat. I feel late. My feet dance at the edge of the curb. The old-style, black MX5 with its music blaring, catches my eye long before I realise it's you in the driving seat. The fluttering of anticipation explodes in my stomach, blinds me to everything that's not you. Now I can't even hear the music that assaults anyone in earshot. You're sassy. Hard arse cool.

I haven't been myself since our wine bar chat. Time plays dangerous tricks on the craving mind. Sleep evaded me. The image of you obsessed my every waking hour. I wondered about *her* too. I'd known my ex was having an affair every time it happened. The changes in behaviour can be subtle, and denial is comforting to the insecure soul, but I knew. Are you deceiving yourself to think *she* doesn't know about your previous exploits? Or is it simply the cost of compromise on her part, the price she's willing to pay to keep you? It doesn't occur to me that she and I might be the same: willing to compromise our needs for your happiness, our sense of security in the balance, our hearts on the line. I feel for her. It's arrogant of me, pre-emptive. She still has you, and there are no guarantees you'll leave her for me.

When you look at me and smile, *she* ceases to exist. You turn the music down and lean over the top of the steering wheel as I clamber into the virtually ground-level car.

"Hi," you say.

Your tone is sultry. Your beaming smile reflects my own, I'm sure. I'm seduced by the sharp scent of the perfume that cause my nostrils to twitch. It's freshly applied, too strong really, but eventually it will mellow and sweeten. It reminds me of being in your office, of the warmth of your body pressed close to me, your lips caressing mine. It's a part of who you are. You identify with that specific scent when really it's another aspect of the façade behind which you seek refuge from *you*, like the Rolex that clinks as your fingers toy with the steering wheel.

"Hi." I click the seat belt into its socket.

You rev the engine, glance across at me, then slam your foot on the accelerator to beat the traffic before the lights turn green.

"I missed you," you say, your eyes flitting between me and the road.

Those words don't touch me. I don't know what that term really means. I've been thinking about you, about us. You're not a possession that I might lose, and the idea of missing you is as alien to me as snow is to the desert. I don't miss my mother. I still love her though. She's still with me in more ways than I could explain. There is nothing to miss. I suppose I'm different from other people in that respect. "Where are we going?"

You give me a sideways glance. I'm sorry that my lack of reciprocation offends you, but I'm not good at saying something if I'm being insincere. I need to recover the situation. "I've been thinking about you," I say.

I watch you keep your eyes on the road. Your mouth twitches though and fine lines try to reach across your temple from the corner of your eye. The fact that they don't make it very far is testament to your youth. You sweep your hair around your pierced ear, showing yourself to me. I'm hooked already, staring, admiring the line of your jaw. Your cheekbones aren't prominent. They're crafted to provide an oval shape to your face, and when you really smile a small dimple appears in your cheek. It's fascinating to watch the transformation. From the sternness of the look I've experienced in your office to the child-like free expression you wear right now.

You're pleased I have been thinking about you. I'm intrigued. Why have you missed me? You barely know me.

The drive takes us out of town. You love speed, don't you? You push the boundaries of the car and the limits on the motorway, and it's still not fast enough. You haven't answered my question about where we're going. We're heading off the M4 toward Windsor. The Union Jack comes into view, high above the castle's walls.

"The Queen is in," you say.

My heart pounds at the thought of serving Queen and country. I think it always will. "Is she expecting us?" I'm being flippant and you chuckle.

We cruise for a time looking for a place to park, then head back out of town to the multi-storey we passed on the way in that had spaces. Your phone rings as we meander down the street. You study the caller's details, reject the call. I think it's *her*. You don't say anything, pocket your phone casually, and obviously feeling undetectable, link your arm through mine.

Scanning the surrounds is a trained response, one that has served me well over the years. I'm acutely aware of what it feels like to avoid being "found out." I don't know if that feeling ever goes away. You seem oblivious even though you have something—someone—to lose. Others might think you brazen. I think you just don't believe you'll get caught. Discomfort of this nature is a familiar friend to me. I heed its message. I'm on high alert for you while we're out in the open, not that I would have a clue who might recognise you. I don't think you notice the tension in my arm, because you don't question me about it.

You lead me to the Thames. You've hired a boat for us. It's a romantic gesture. I observe you as you effortlessly seduce the man with your charisma. His eyes are all over your body, then linger at your breasts. He's beside himself with excitement, and before he knows it he's extended our boat hire to the end of the day at no extra cost. How did you do that? You dismiss him the moment you've struck the deal, and he doesn't even notice he's been castrated. I hold up my hand to him in thanks, and he waves politely to me. It's you he's interested in, but you've already turned your back on him. You grab my hand, yank me unceremoniously onto the narrow deck, and unhook the ropes from the mooring. You've done this before, haven't you? Was it with your other lovers? The thought is a fleeting one. I dismiss it as you dismissed the boat seller a moment ago. We are the same, you and me. We know how to get what we want, and we're not going to distract the mission with irrelevance.

It's quiet further down the river on the outskirts of Windsor. You guide the craft with the lightest touch, our movement slow and steady on the still water. The Union Jack hangs limp and lifeless in the absence of the breeze. It is a visual anchor point, not that we need one. The river only goes in two directions.

You're gazing at me and then you smile. "Tell me about you."

I'm stumped. There's nothing to say.

You give me your best therapist look, though the softness in your gaze tells me you're asking me out of genuine interest. I'm not used to sharing or talking about me, and I don't know where to start. Nor do I want to. I tell you about my father, simply because he had come to mind that time when we were in your office. "My father wasn't a bad man. He was an alcoholic."

You frown and tilt your head slightly.

"The two aren't the same thing," I say. "Though the alcoholic's behaviour can devastate the lives of those they love. It's my belief that people aren't in control of themselves when they're gripped by the addiction," I say. "It's archetypal." I tell you how I reconciled my thoughts about his behaviour. That I shifted my emotion from anger to forgiveness, through compassion. Staring at you, it strikes me how natural it feels talking to you about the man who left his mark on my body. I've never spoken to anyone about this before. But here now, with you, something stirred in me. Comfort. Security. Maybe knowing you'll relate to the trauma inflicted on young minds by ignorant parents.

You raise your eyebrows, widening your eyes, and then pull your upper lip between your teeth.

I continue with my theory. "Addicts are trying to numb the pain, avoid feelings they can't handle, manage a life they're ill-equipped to deal with. Blaming them doesn't resolve anything. It's like saying someone who is mentally ill has the capacity to handle stress when they can't even work out how to get dressed of a morning."

I'm not condoning any behaviour, simply empathising with the truth. I know that if I had lived my father's life, if I had been him in his world and experienced all that he had, I would have been an aggressive alcoholic too. Whether I'm right or wrong is irrelevant to my argument. What's important is that thinking the way I do has allowed me to forgive him, to love him beyond his destructive actions. I'm not angry with him. I don't pity him, but I do feel sorry for him. I think he forgot he had a choice. It's difficult for the addict to take responsibility for themselves and much easier to vent anger on the world, blame others for their pain. It's totally natural to repeat the patterns, the programming they've been carved from and lash out at a world they can't navigate. It's the abused that becomes the abuser. Locked in a web of destruction that brings them down with their prey. I would have loved to know his rationale. But he's long since dead, and I wouldn't have been able to get the answers to my questions when he was alive. I shrug and stare at you.

"Sometimes we need to accept the things in others that we cannot change. Understanding them doesn't mean we have to agree with them or act like them, but we do need to dig deep to unlearn those things we see in them that we don't like in ourselves, don't you think? Searching for answers, for revenge, for apologies can eat away at us like cancer. We don't know that cancer exists in us, and yet it drives every thought, feeling, and behaviour. We can spend a lifetime searching and forget to live. Sometimes we need to accept things at face value, don't you think?"

"I think people need answers," you say.

You would. You're the therapist, and many of your clients need to know why they are broken. "And when they get them, how does that help? What does it change?" In my mind, they're not broken. They're navigating life with the deck of cards they've been dealt. They simply need to learn how to play. It's not easy, I know that. But it *is* possible, and as long as possibility exists, there's always hope. Hope transforms lives.

You seem to go inside your mind, search the chasm of your understanding, and debate with your own need for resolutions.

"With answers people can let go of the past and move on."

I like your conviction, misguided though it is. "Answers can destroy people." That also must be true. It's the duality, you see. As rain is essential to the creation of life, so too it has the power to eliminate that which it has created. Answers have the power to heal and the power to destroy. Context is what matters. "What would happen if we were able to thrive, flow with the fog of uncertainty, with no need for answers, no desire for resolution?"

Your nose flares. You have no words. You feel threatened, but that's not my intention. I find the debate interesting, but it's touched a nerve in you. Maybe I'm delusional in what I believe human beings are capable of, but I've seen incredible strength manifest from the embers of human destruction. The fathers who forgave those who slayed their sons and raped their daughters in the name of liberation. This is an extreme case, I know. You're right too, people will always need answers while they lack faith. My theory is hypothetical, of course. I like to philosophise.

I smile.

You're staring at me, and then my lightness registers and your features soften.

"Do you want a glass of wine?" you ask.

I frown. Your smile grows, and your eyes retrieve their sparkle.

"There's a fridge at the back."

I take that as a command, leap to my feet, and stumble to the back of the boat which oscillates with my movement.

The fridge is stacked with the buffet you asked the rental company to provide. Ham, cheese, prawns, lobster, salad. You've covered all the possible taste bases. Scored a home run there, my love. A bowl of freshly cut fruit brimming with kiwi, papaya, melon, and strawberries sits on the worktop next to a small farmhouse loaf of freshly baked bread. There aren't many cupboards to search so locating the corkscrew and glasses is a quick process. The cork slides from the bottle with an ease that is fitting for the vintage Chablis inside. The familiar pop is a delicious reminder of what is to come, the aroma set free. I pour two glasses, return the bottle to the fridge, and make my way slowly back to you.

Your face is taut. You're looking at the messages on your phone.

"Everything okay?"

You hadn't been aware of me, and my words jolt you.

"Yes."

You take the glass. I sit opposite you, the sun on my face. Even in the tension that surrounds you, I feel close. It's hard to explain. I have no theory, no reference point from which I can label my feelings. It's a sense of knowing that's absolute. At this moment you could have been a serial killer, and I would've still been in love with you. I would've still seen *you* beneath the veil of self-preservation.

"Do you want to talk?"

Your top lip quivers, and your eyes quickly become glassy. Though you are looking directly at me, you don't see me.

"How do you tell someone you love that it's over?"

The words slice through my heart instantly. I know it's a terminal wound though I feel no pain. Then I realise you're referring to *her*. The reboot brings my senses back to me in a rush of blood that kicks off the throbbing between my legs. I don't know how to answer you, but I know you've chosen me. "It's tough," I say.

Tears fall gracelessly, unashamedly onto your cheeks. You're trembling as you sip the wine and wipe the tears with the back of your hand.

I reach into my pocket and hand over the only tissue I have. I've only used it once, I say. You snigger through snot. I know that nothing I say can heal the pain. It's no one's fault, though that won't temper the guilt you feel knowing the hurt you're going to inflict on her. It's not even about me, not really. But for a decision, it could be another woman, or even a man, you're having this conversation with.

This is the flow of life in all its wonder, the bitter and the sweet, the love and the loss. I've come to realise that the gaps we need filling for us to feel whole will always seek the source that can sustain them. When that source runs dry, they will hunt down a new supplier. I take your hand in mine and squeeze. It's the life jacket that tells you, you will survive the storm.

You hang on, gather your thoughts, take control of your emotions. It's not the time for smiling and laughing, but you emit a gentle laugh that's riddled with desperation. A cry for help.

"I love you," I say.

You look into my eyes.

I swallow though my mouth is parched from speaking my truth.

I've loved you since I first set eyes on you.

I've never loved anyone as I love you.

These are the thoughts that have haunted me since that auspicious day I rocked up to your training course. I think you love me too.

You're shaking your head, toying with your top lip.

"How do you know that?"

The question taps a sensitivity button, and I flinch inside. You wouldn't have known the impact. I might not experience anger, or sadness, or guilt in swathes as some do, as you do, but I know intimately the beating of my heart. I shrug. "I just know," I say.

You finish your drink in a long swig. I go and get the bottle.

When I return, you're leaning back, facing the sun with your eyes closed. You would look asleep if it wasn't for the tension in your jaw and neck. Your eyes flick open in my shadow.

"You look tired," I say.

"Thanks," you say.

You take the glass and then a long slug of the wine.

I sit with my back to the sun, sip my drink. You like the sour wines, don't you? "Are you sure?" I ask.

You shake your head, and the tears come again.

"Then don't say anything to her."

You look at me as if I've just said something so incomprehensible, so insane that I wonder if I've missed something. Then you're looking me up and down but not in an explicitly lustful way. You're taking me in, holding the idea of being with me in a bubble in your mind.

"I can't deny you."

Your words take my breath away. I nod. I know that feeling.

You seem relieved and look across the river to the shades of orange and gold lining the bank. I love the leaves in autumn, and this year is particularly colourful.

When you turn back to face me, fire flashes from your eyes.

"I've never wanted anyone like I want you," you say.

Your tone reflects your carnal desires. I'm trembling from the inside out, and it's thrown my sense of propriety. The urgency is too strong to resist. I don't know how soon we will lie together, but I know it will be before the day is out.

I'm not proud of the fact that we're in an affair.

I can't deny you either.

I won't deny you.

I'm in love with you.

10.

Our first time together was passionate, yes, but frantic. It was over too fast. We were both too hungry. You'd dispatched our clothes to the floor within seconds of entering the room. You like to dominate, don't you? You grabbed my hand and dragged me quickly to the bathroom. The chill of the tiles stung my back. I felt the emotional distance through which you live as you entered me. We hadn't even kissed. Your eyelids were closed, shielding your thoughts from me. Denying the truth? You weren't really with me, were you? Were you thinking of *her*?

I think you were lost in illusion, driven by your past experiences, and craving a feeling. When I came in your hand, you opened your eyes, and your smile conveyed pleasure. Power. Achievement. And then your lips claimed mine, sealing the deal. You were still hungry. You led me to the bed, and we fucked hard, disregarding tenderness for sexual gratification. Raw, laced with frustration for you, guilt for me. After, I lay on the bed confused. You slept like a baby for a few hours, and when you woke you kissed me with a tenderness that settled my heart. We rose before dawn and travelled back to London.

You seemed happy.

You promised you were going to tell her about us.

I didn't hear from you for days after that. I sat in the park in the cold, waiting, watching your office from time to time, wondering about you, worried about *her*. Then I went back to work. I'd been assigned to a new family. Their needs weren't exacting. The girl's name was Charlotte. She'd just been discovered by a record label after turning sixteen. From what I could see, she was more in need of the parent figure she lacked while her biological ones swanned the seas on their thirty-million pound super yacht.

I wasn't expecting the knock at the door late on that Wednesday evening. You were lucky. It was my night off.

My heart jumps into my throat when I see you.

Your skin is ashen, your puffy eyes deep-set in shadow. You stare at me with a sadness that runs so deep it must have journeyed through generations. Your lips are pale, dry, and quivering, and when you abandon your suitcase at the door and fall into my arms, you are full-on shivering. The scent of you and the softness you exude when vulnerable is so enthralling. I hold you tightly, and we stand allowing the warmth to penetrate us both until your breathing steadies.

"You told her," I whisper.

I feel your head rocking against my chest, though I already know the answer. I breathe you in, nestle my face into your hair. For a brief moment, anxiety pinches me. I reason with its concerns and the feeling subsides. I tell myself, whatever might happen next, we will face it together. Then the niggling feeling reminds me I've never managed to live in close proximity with anyone. I close my eyes, kiss your head, hold you reassuringly in my arms, and release a deep breath. "It'll be okay," I whisper.

Your head rocks against my chest again, then you ease back and gaze at me. "I didn't mean for things to turn out this way," you say.

I shrug. I'm not really sure what you expected would happen after telling her you wanted to be with another woman. That was never going to go down well, even if she had reached the end of the road with you. It's a control issue for some people. You look so fucking destroyed, though, and my heart is melting my logic faster than a heat wave thaws ice. "Come in, Justine."

You take the few short paces from my door to the living room. I plonk your bag on the inside of the flat and silently shut the door to your old life. Of course, she's kicked you out. I've been there, remember? It was your girlfriend's house, your girlfriend's rich parent's money that supported you both, you tell me.

"I have nothing," you say.

"You have me."

"I didn't mean it that way. All I have is in my car, and what's in that suitcase."

I shrug. I can't see the problem with that. My one-bedroom flat is small, but I have few possessions. There's space for you. "You can stay here," I say.

You're comparing. The cosy two-seater sofa, a box-television sat on the only other piece of furniture in the room, the open plan layout that situates the kitchen in the same room. No doubt it pales against the palace you've just walked away from. It's natural. You haven't adjusted to the reality of what you've done. You've ended what you had, and you're at the beginning of something you didn't know you were getting into until your heart refused to follow the old rules.

You're shit scared.

So am I.

"Would you like a drink?" I ask.

You nod. I cup your cheek softly, draw your eyes to look into mine. I'm trying to reach the *you* inside you. "I need to nip to the shop," I whisper.

You start to shake.

"I won't be long. Come." I take your hand, lead you past the front door, and show you the bedroom and the bathroom. "Make yourself at home. Unpack, run a bath. I'll be five minutes, tops." I'm nodding to encourage you to affirm the plan.

You blink and allow a tight smile to form. "Okay."

I grab my coat and head out the door, run to the local off-licence, and choose the coldest wine they have out of the small fridge and a bottle of Jack Daniels from the shelf behind the counter. The wine is some shitty brand I know can't compete with the Chablis you're accustomed to, and I haven't drunk JD in a long time. I grab two Cornish pasties from the chiller. They'll taste like plastic, and I don't know if you'll want anything to eat. I'm not hungry for food. It's the best I can do without heading for the supermarket and getting back to you is my priority over nutritional value.

By the time I reach the door to my flat, my heart is racing. Not from the jogging, but an anticipation of a future together has filtered into my awareness and claimed its place. Exhilaration courses through my veins. You really are in my flat, in my life, with me. Yes, it's early days. Yes, this feeling scares the fuck out of me. But it's also the most significant thing I have ever experienced. It's surreal. I know as is with any mission, the battle may be won but there's still the extraction plan to execute, and that will come with a new set of challenges. You may not have much to physically withdraw from the house, but there'll be the emotional fall-out to contend with. I told you before, remember, I'm not devoid of emotion. I'm not detached. I just don't hang on to feelings, especially the negative ones. Guilt is going to haunt you for a while, I think.

The scent of my body wash is in the air, and the idea of it on you makes me smile. You've managed to turn on the stereo in the bedroom too. Sade's *Diamond Life* is one of my favourite all-time albums. I take our provisions into the kitchen, pour you a large glass of wine and me a JD, and amble into the bathroom. You look at ease with your eyes closed and your head back, your hands toying with the foamy bubbles. You have a good voice, I think. I lean against the door frame and take pleasure from your enjoyment of the song, *Smooth Operator*. The lyrics fall softly from your lips. You know every word, and only when the song comes to an end do you open your eyes and see me. You blush slowly, slink down in the bath, duck your head under the water, and come up laughing.

It makes me laugh too. "What?" I say and shrug.

Your smile is sweet. You've always been here, haven't you? You rub the water from your face. I hand over the glass, watch you drink, and take a sip of my own.

When you look at me, your heart is open and your mind is quiet. You're *with* me, connected, in an exquisite moment of bliss that I want us to hold onto forever. I could die now and know I had truly loved and felt love in equal measure. It's so at odds with our first time together. There's no hysterical need to fuck right now, and yet when that feeling does arise later, I'm sure it will be so much richer this time around. There will be no feverish rapidity driving our passion, but there will be no absence of desire.

This is me.

I know you feel it too. Vulnerability is free in the suspension of fear, and the absolute sense of trust brings wholeness.

This is the state of being at one with another. I'd never experienced it before this moment.

"Come in," you say.

I put my glass on the side of the bath, strip from my clothes, and join you. You part your legs so I can sit, but I want to face you. I want to observe you and hold onto this bubble of ecstasy in which we're floating together.

You are so beautiful.

We stare into each other's eyes, and there's no doubt we are thinking the same thoughts, because we groan in the same tone of voice at exactly the same moment in time. We smirk knowingly, both programmed by the unwritten sensory code that will guide the next few hours of our life. Silently we stand, step out of the bath, dry, and walk into the bedroom.

There is no person to make the first move, no person to touch first, no first anything between us. We pass seamlessly, synchronously, through the never-ending exchange that is the peak of sensual intimacy. I explore your smooth skin with a delicate touch, enjoying the way the flesh puckers around your erect nipples with my perceptive tongue. I'm learning the language of *you*. You like to be submissive more than you would admit. Gentleness touches you profoundly. Has anyone made love to you with such tenderness before? I'm in no rush. I have a lifetime with you.

Your skin tastes of slightly salted caramel. Every stroke of my tongue teases your senses, and the quiet rhythm builds in fleeting bursts of tension that spasm within you. I challenge you with a new sensation, expose your neck, and graze my teeth along its length. I sense your throbbing pulse increase in pace at the tip of my tongue. I come to your mouth, linger a while. I can't help it. I love kissing you. Your lips are so silky soft. When our tongues explore, no one is leading. There is no force, no pushing and pulling. It's instinctive. Balanced. We know how we fit together. No one is plotting, there's no evaluation of impact. We are simply being, navigating without judgement, reacting, and responding in effortless harmony.

We are not seeking a feeling. We are living the most precious gift given to us.

Love.

This love is like nothing else. It has no destructive power.

It's a constant. It's captured in the words crafted by the poet. It's the essence that psychological theories cannot explain. Its existence is debated by philosophers. Spiritual gurus spend years in dedicated practice to know it. The addict shoots up to reach this place of being.

This is not sexual, and nothing compares to it.

You cannot seek it, because it can't be found. It's elusive, you see, and it appears when you least expect it. When you're not trying. You cannot hold onto it, and you may never experience it again. But once you have sensed it, you have known love intimately.

You are transformed.

It's disarming, and when we come in each other's arms, eyes locked in deep embrace, we both feel it.

You look like a rabbit caught in the headlights, and it makes me chuckle. You didn't expect that, did you? The profundity confounds you, messes with your mind. You lost control, didn't you? You ceded effortlessly in the moment you accepted your vulnerability. You trusted me, flowed with me. This wasn't an act of submission. That's way too deliberate. This was beyond volition. It was an opening of our hearts to each other. Without expectation, without judgement, evaluation, or critical interpretation. Importantly, it was unconditional. We became lost in one exquisite, precious moment in time.

Your eyes are still wide open. Tears are filling them and flowing onto your cheeks. And then you awaken to your thoughts. Fear of rejection clutters your mind, and the only outcome possible for us is a broken heart. Tension slowly encroaches on your face and into your jaw until normality is restored. The guards have been despatched, and they close the gates to your heart. I want to say to you, "It's too fucking late, my love." Fear has inflicted the fatal wound to your heart, not the act of love that we just shared.

I study your eyes and smile, savour what remains of the flicker of openness before the light dims completely. Even though the guards have resumed their post and will protect your heart at any cost, I know I will always love you.

I gave myself to you too, you see.

You didn't know then that that was a first for me too.

My heart skips to a new beat. It's yours.

11.

When I slipped out of our bed in the early hours of the morning, you were sleeping as soundly as a baby. You looked at peace. I left you a note as I have done each day for the past week. *I will be back late. I love you.* When I return after another uneventful day with the precocious sixteen-year-old would-be superstar, I can still smell you on me as I close the door behind me. I feel taller than my five-feet-nine inches, warmer than my thirty-seven degrees. My visual acuity is heightened, my gait is athletic.

I am alive.

You're curled up, sobbing quietly on the sofa, and I run to you. I fall to my knees, pull you close to me, hold you tight. "What's wrong, my love?"

"She's threatening to report me," you say.

"For what?" I was being flippant, I know. We hadn't done anything wrong though. I didn't understand.

"You were my client," you say.

I roll my eyes. I was never your client in my mind, and I certainly wasn't your client when we got together. "That's bollocks."

You stroke my cheek, but you're not smiling. You wear a look of concern that would win the scariest mask in a masked ball contest. It's intense, and there's no doubting the stress behind it that subjugates your thoughts.

"It's against protocol, Claire."

"Fuck protocol." I've never been one for senseless rules.

You remind me that transference and counter-transference must be taken seriously in your business. It's too easy to get close to a client and mistake it for something that it isn't. But you're not talking about you and me, are you?

I can see that it might be a problem for some people. Needy people. I'm not one of those. "What does she want?"

"Me to leave the practice."

"She's blackmailing you?"

"Yes."

I flinch. I'm not angry. I'm fascinated at the lengths some people will reach to exact revenge, to punish another because they've been hurt. I don't understand what purpose that behaviour serves. Does she really feel good for doing something deliberately destructive? You falling in love with me wasn't deliberate. The two things are qualitatively different, chalk and cheese.

I assume you will fight her, so I ask, "You want me to find someone to take her out?" I'm joking, but you look at me oddly. "Sorry."

"You're not taking this seriously, are you?"

"What are you going to do?"

"I have to leave."

It hasn't dawned on me that this is such a big deal for you. In the military we moved around a lot, and in my current work my client could change at any time. Mobility is my normality. It's for everyone's protection.

I watch your focus shift inwards in the narrowing of your eyes, the thinning of your lips. This is uncomfortable for you. "Why don't you open your own clinic?"

You shake your head. "I'm going to need to leave the industry, Claire."

I frown. This doesn't compute with me at all. "Why?" I hear irritation in the tone of my voice. I'm pissed for you. You worked so hard to build your reputation, and you're a good therapist.

Your eyes search skywards. "She'll report me, Claire. I need to take time out, or there's a chance I could get struck off."

"Shit! Because of us?"

"Yes."

I'm not thinking about the money, but you are. You hastily pace the short distance across the living room and back, repeatedly. You're making me dizzy. You're upset, and I feel it in a dull ache in the bottom of my heart. I want to help take the pain away.

"What if we move out of town? Could you set up on your own?"

You are shaking your head, and your boots clunk heavily on the hardwood floor as you take four steps, turn, take four steps, turn. I think reality is dawning, because you look as if you're going to implode. The situation feels unjust to me too. You can't just walk away from the career you've worked so hard to achieve. She got the dogs, the cat, and the fish, and that's not enough.

She wants to bury you.

Wow. That's the ugly side of humanity. I genuinely feel compassion for *her* though. *Her* world has been turned upside down by something she feels is outside of *her* control. She feels betrayed by you. Whether she actually wanted to be with you or not, she didn't end the relationship. You did, and now she feels the need to claim her power back. If you considered my perception, you would think I was betraying you, us. I'm not. I just see *her* too.

*****

You resign, of course. You have no choice.

I put my flat on the market. The vendor tells us it will sell quickly.

You consider your options. You could set up in private practice where no one will know you. Take your name off the governing body's qualified therapist list. It's a bit of a backward step. Private clients are hard to acquire. Doctors won't work with you if you're not accredited. You have no references, no testimonials that demonstrate your competence. It will cost money that we don't have to set up. Then there's the question of where to go.

We settle on Reading, an hour on the train to London. I would've preferred somewhere closer.

You explore the possibilities for a walk-in clinic, strike a deal with the local health and wellbeing shop, and get leaflets printed. You're in business. We spend the evenings searching online for a three-bed house just out of town. I let you narrow down the options, there are only four in the end, and you choose the best one because you seem to have a strong idea of what you need.

If it makes you happy, I'm happy.

You pick the Georgian-styled property with small leaded windows. I think it'll be dark inside. You think it's got character. You're right. It's quaint.

And, it's dark inside.

The third bedroom will make a great office, the second bedroom a clinic room. The flat sells quickly, as the agent promised, and we put an offer in on the Georgian semi. It's rejected. You're pissed about that and offer over the asking price. When you really want something, you go hell for leather to get it, don't you?

We'll be packing up in a few weeks and moving to Reading. We don't have a lot of furniture to shift so we will hire a van and do it ourselves. You're excited. We splash out on a bottle of champagne to celebrate. I have to go to the supermarket to get a second. Life is good. Sex is...hot, frantic, and physical. You prefer it that way. It's safer.

We're high on life, high on champagne, high on that feeling. The timing is right I think, so I ask about the future. I want to get married, but you're not that fussed. You want kids, I'm easy either way.

We'll end up doing both in a couple of years.

You will cry as you say your vows.

I will weep at the image of the racing heartbeat nestled inside your womb.

You need to meet my parents, you say as we start the second bottle.

I suppose. I tilt my glass for you to fill it.

You've already told me what an arsehole your dad is and that neither him nor your mother support the fact that you're gay. He's a misogynistic prick, you say. I shake my head at the conviction in your tone. I'm really looking forward to meeting him...not.

Your parents hoped she was a passing phase, didn't they? Now there's another woman in your life who's here to stay. You find it funny. You're winning the battle against them, aren't you? They're incensed at what they consider your brazen irreverence of normality, of God. Fuck them, you say. You really don't like them much, do you? And yet, you're clearly bound to them.

I'm sure it's hard for a parent. After meeting them, I too say, fuck them.

What gives them the right to dictate your life just because you were once their child? You're an adult now, capable of making your own choices and taking responsibility for your decisions.

They can't understand why you left your job. Leaving me would've been preferable. They blame me for your situation of course and make no bones about telling you what you should do next. Reading is further away from them. They're not happy. I'm beginning to warm to Reading. I listen as they regale their own achievements. No one does it better than them, do they? You slouch at the dining table, silently chewing on your frustration, swallowing your rage. Your posture reveals the pain learned long ago, suffering that clings to the blood running through your veins. The agony, the lie, the guilt, the shame: the cocktail is far more destructive to your sense of self-worth than I could ever imagine. I get drunk. We excuse ourselves from the table and leave them to drink themselves into a stupor. They do that with practiced perfection.

The bedroom is dark, the sheets cold. You resist me touching you out of a sense of child-like adherence to their rules and respect for their sensitivities. Then as you drift, you dream, and your warm hand slides between my hot legs. You're half asleep, shifting in and out of awareness. It's an exquisite state. We fuck hard, and I cover your mouth with my hand to stop you screaming out as you orgasm. You're not as trained in the art of silent sex as I am. It's exhilarating. It's passionate. It's sexual gratification at its peak.

We move to Reading, and it's another eight months before we see your parents again. It comes around too soon for my liking. A lot has happened in our lives in that time, and you're excited to share the most important bit of our news with them.

You raise your glass of champagne in a toast and grin broadly.

"You're going to be grandparents."

Your words land like Hiroshima, and I can't help but think we will feel the fallout for years to come.

The smile swiftly slides from your beautiful face as the visual assault whipped across the room from them to you. They have no respect for your feelings, do they? I squeeze your hand, but you don't feel me. You're lost in the umbilical cord that connects you as family. At that moment, you are conditioned to see only them, to hear only them.

"What?" They yell in unison.

His voice is deep, hers has that irritatingly high-pitched squeak. They couldn't be more opposite. The shock doesn't stop them both emptying their drink down their throats and refilling their glasses though, does it? Any excuse.

Anger accosts me with the grip of a tornado, sweeps me up, carries me along, and creates turmoil that has no exit route. I stand up for you in a fit of blind rage that possesses me like nothing I have ever known. I surprise myself. I surprise you. They think me rude. That's fucking ironic. It doesn't stop them continuing to voice their vitriolic opinion about our joyous situation.

They continue to jibe at you, at us, at everything we aspire to become. I get drunk again. You protect our baby.

Lying in bed later, holding hands, we laugh at their melodrama.

"It's the only time they have ever agreed on something," you say.

It would have been funny had their impact not been so cruel.

They were indeed united in their disdain. I understood they had landed a blow on you of the most vicious kind. I had watched you revert to the child in their presence. You became the frog that floats merrily in the pot of water unaware that it is being slowly heated. They have you in their grasp, and they sure as hell aren't going to let you go—and especially not to someone like me. It's their way of protecting you, of course. But I think they're killing you, because you're much more than they could ever be.

I am your protector now, not them.

They had their chance. Fucked it up royally, I discovered later.

They can't let you be you, can they?

Their rejection slips through your defences with the grace of a hot knife through butter. I confess to you that I was struck dumb by the wrath that ensued. They're beyond stubborn, aren't they? In my mind, any God-figure I might consider subscribing to would bless our decision to bring children into this world not vilify us for it. I couldn't imagine disregarding my child's choices out of a sense of loyalty to a bigoted belief structure that would, without question, destroy that same child. It's so ludicrous to me as to be inconceivable.

Your friends also reckon our relationship happened too quickly. Why is it that those who surround you are so quick to tell you what you're doing is wrong? Look in the mirror, I would say to them. Those who live in glass houses shouldn't throw stones. Yes, I know some of the biblical phrases. I went to Sunday school as a child, and I will wield the ones that suit my argument. I feel fortunate. I don't have friends like you.

Your friends don't even know you, let alone me. They don't see *you*. They think your world reflects their own dull, inane existence. They must think that way, of course, because being different threatens them. It's the dark side of our competitive instinct, where one person's success illuminates another's failure. If you're happy in your life, how can they validate their own happiness living a different life? They are the athlete who has to cheat to win. They are the politician happy taking the bribes. They are the parent who always knows what's right for their offspring. It's their ego striving to feel powerful. Better than the rest is the only measure of success. I think a lot of people struggle with difference. They prefer people who are like them. It makes life easier, more comfortable.

"We're not like them," I say.

Ours isn't a fairy tale romance.

It's far more than that.

We're soul mates.

We came together a million light-years ago and made a promise to find each other in this new world. We have known the essence of each other over many lifetimes.

We're meant to be together now.

This is our time. I believe that is true, and so do you.

What they believe, what the others think, it doesn't matter to me. Does it matter to you? Stress applies pressure on a relationship in many ways we begin to discover. Who needs friends and family to add to that?

12.

Reading grows on me. Though the trek into London every day is a ball-ache, it's worth it. The suburbs are tranquil, so quiet by comparison with the bustle of the city where even the park in which I used to sit and wait for you is now a cacophony to my delicate countryfied ears. In our small back garden, we have the soft rush of the wind sifting through the trees and the stillness of night hangs in mute darkness. I'm obsessed with the sunrise at this time of year. I watch in awe, the oranges and reds expanding and becoming brilliant white, as the sun rises every morning when I'm on the train into town.

This is me.

But you are lonely. I'm working double shifts to pay off the re-mortgage we took out on the house to pay for the artificial insemination treatments.

It's the middle of the night when the sound of you heaving draws me from sleep. You're not beside me. You're in the en-suite, and I hear you start weeping. You don't need to tell me you've miscarried. There's something I can't explain, but I'm smothered by the feeling that life was being extinguished, being drained from you. And in doing so, was draining from me too.

I go to you, though you hate having anyone around when you're throwing up, and lead you back to our bed.

Empty, raw, you lay in the space next to me, and the convulsions grip you until the point sleep takes you.

I try to hold you in my arms, comfort you, but you reject my touch. I understand. Sleep evades me that night. Work was tougher as a result.

Loss changes our relationship to life, I think.

We never got to see the colour of their eyes.

We never got to know whether they were a he or she, to watch their character shaped through the cheeky smile on their face.

The pulsing beat of light on the radiographer's screen at six-weeks looked fine.

But nature knows best, and devastatingly, it stripped us of hope.

But hope is a resilient emotion. Perhaps the most powerful emotion we have as human beings. We will try again.

The sadness I'd seen in your eyes the first time I met you now casts its long shadow over us both. Your work follows the profile of your desire, slowly decreasing to the point that you stop taking referrals and encourage your clients to move on. Two women refuse to be palmed off onto another therapist, and they remain with you, but you see them in the café down the road rather than our house. We put a double bed in the second bedroom.

How does the therapist admit they need help? It's a sign of weakness, isn't it? You go and see the doctor, take the prescription from his hand, and then file it in the pile of paper in your office. I recognise the stubbornness, it's hard not to. Your parents don't see the problem.

I come home one day for you to tell me that your mother has said, "It's for the best, darling," over the phone. It was a good job I'd been at work when she called, or I would have driven all the way to their house and done something stupid. I punch the wall, and it takes me back to life with my father all those years ago. I would punch the wall harder then, and then when my fists bled, I would use the back of my head until my ears rang and silent tears streamed down my face. The anger I felt at the time of those beatings reappears like the phoenix rising from the ashes. I feel it surge at my frustration with the injustice. I've never cared about someone as much as I care about you. I'm incensed that they could be so flippant with your heart. It confuses me that you think she is worthy of your time, your love. "Why do you still speak to her every day?"

"She's my mother."

"So?" I've never subscribed to the blood is thicker than water myth. My closest friends in the military have meant far more to me over the years. They had been there while my father lay dying in the hospital bed, unable to verbalise a response to whether he wanted a cup of tea or not. Cirrhosis of the liver is a painful way to go. My mum had been a friend to me, so she doesn't count as family. She would never speak to me as your mother does to you. Never.

The biggest kicker for me comes a month after the third miscarriage. I come home late from work, and the only thought on my mind is a hot bath and warm bed.

You surprise me. I thought you'd be in bed. Instead, you're sat on the sofa in the dark, a glass of wine in your shaking hand.

I approach you with open arms.

You shake your head violently, the look in your eyes wild and empty.

The distance you've created moves like ice down my spine.

"Our relationship's not working," you say.

Fuck. As magnets repel, the words catapult me into the middle of the room. I must have a deranged look on my face if my thoughts are anything to go by. Confusion isn't accurate. Confusion suggests that different truths exist, and one is undecided about which truth applies. Flabbergasted doesn't even come close either. That word has too positive a feel about it. This is an unprovoked attack from an ally. There is no greater betrayal than that which comes from the enemy within.

The sharp blade of the knife penetrates my heart instantly, twists slowly, and the essence of life drains from me. I'm grappling for my thoughts. I'm shaking. And then the rage ignites the tiredness in me, and the fighter emerges in full force. "What the fuck do you mean?"

You're snivelling and shaking your head. How much had you had to drink? You rarely slur your words, so it's hard to tell.

"We aren't working," you say again.

A second blade to the gut. "What?"

Maybe I sounded like your parents when they responded to being told you were pregnant, because you look at me like thunder had just become an alien and taken you over.

This is the beginning of a major storm.

It's my fault, apparently. All of it. The fact that you had to leave your job in London. The fact that your parents don't like me. The fact that we had mortgaged ourselves to the hilt for the AI treatments, and interest rates were now hitting an all-time high. The fact that we'd lost our chance of a baby. The fact that you would be unlikely to conceive again, so the consultant had told us.

"You don't love me," you say.

That fucking hurt. "Of course I do." My heart is burning in desperation, my legs are going to give way, and my head is filling with toxic thought. It's an onslaught. I can't breathe, I can't think, I can't digest. I need to slow my pulse and take the heat out of the situation. You're depressed, I remind myself, but you're relentlessly beating me with your disdain.

This isn't you, is it?

Those four words, *you don't love me*, ricochet around my mind like the proverbial stone in a well of loneliness. Deep down, I don't believe you feel that way, but hurt chips at my faith in us, contests everything in my world that means anything. You are my everything. It feels like a piece of my heart is in atrophy, dying slowly.

Some might say, I'd been naïve to think you and me were on the same page as far as love goes. I am different, I know. They may be right. But, we'd shared the most intimate feeling possible between two people, remember? That you would challenge my love for you was beyond my concept of reality.

I stay in the second bedroom that night, though sleep evaded me on and off for weeks. There's a distance between us now, and I have no vessel in which to navigate my way back to you. It was like the Titanic went down, and me…you…us drowned in it.

I wonder if this is the dark night of the soul you're going through? The point of transformation that will destroy that which is broken within you, so *you* can finally blossom.

I'm hopeful.

***

"If you don't believe in you, how can you ever believe in us? I can't fill your fucking gaps any more than you can fill mine."

Your gaze is vacant, the lines on your forehead prominent even though we've had this conversation many times before this moment. You want that good feeling back, and it's eluding you. You resent me, because I'm not suffering. You blame me, because I'm not enough right now, because, I can't make you happy.

"I told you, I'm not perfect. I will let you down," I say.

You'd thought I was joking when I said this the first time around, but now you know I wasn't. I saw you. I anticipated this moment would arise. You've always had the capacity to

103

break my heart. I just didn't have a fucking clue what that would feel like.

I'm dying here, and I want you to find the strength to come with me.

My heart is begging you. Please, see me. Please, be with *me*.

By morning the pain had defused in you. You're putting coffee grounds into the filter, the local radio station screaming out some popular song with no lyrics. You're singing though, excited, inspired by something that had lifted you between our last conversation and now.

I am drained. Confused. Lost.

You smile and pull my limp body into a warm embrace.

"I've always wanted to be an architect."

I didn't know that. I can't, won't, hug you back, and when you let me go, I nod. "We'll make it work," I say softly.

You aren't thinking about the cost of your next venture, but I am. With hollowness residing in my heart and desolation lining my gut and suffocating the flames of joy I had been blessed to feel, I put on my coat. I gaze in your direction, and the pain of the previous evening reflects back. "I won't be home tonight. It's Charlotte's eighteenth birthday, and I need to be there."

Your eyes are locked onto your phone. You haven't heard me.

I'll text you later to make sure you aren't expecting me home for supper.

13.

You're enjoying your studies, I think. You talked about it in the early days, but I've been working long hours and sleeping in the second bedroom so as not to disturb you. The living room is looking nice since you redecorated. I didn't know you were going to do that. The whitewashed walls really brighten up the dark space. It smells clean and fresh.

We walk in silence through to the kitchen. You sip from your wine like an excited puppy, fill me a glass, and hand it over.

"I'm going to tackle the bedroom next. I'm thinking apple green will go well with the dark pine furniture."

I'm clueless with colour, so there's no point in consulting me. I nod. "Sounds good." I think the ambivalence comes through in my voice.

I take a long sip of the perfectly chilled Chablis, willing it to numb the heartache I feel in your presence.

Love shouldn't hurt this badly.

Should it?

Is this the duality at play? Love and loss?

We amble into the garden. You sit in the shade of the apple tree. I close my eyes and will the sun to comfort me. Warm summer evenings sooth the tired soul, so they say. The wine helps lift my spirits, too. It's a norm I'm uncomfortable with, but I'm riding the waves with you. I open my eyes, locate your gaze. "How's the course going?" I ask.

"He's an interior designer by career."

You continue to talk animatedly about how talented your new teacher is. You're thinking of switching to study Interior Design. It's more your thing.

"That's good." I close my eyes again and breathe deeply.

"I'm thinking about the possibility of finding a house renovation project. A buy-to-let kind of thing or something we could do up and sell on. We can make money," you say.

I nod. "Where are you thinking of finding a place?" There isn't a chance in hell of that kind of project in this neck of the woods, and we don't have the money.

"I'm not sure."

I know you'll research it later, then fall asleep and wake up inspired.

You stride into the kitchen and return with skewered meat for the barbeque. The sizzling alerts my stomach before the aroma reaches me. I go to the fridge, then refill our glasses. You toss the meat on the griddle and sip your drink.

"I have to go to Germany, by the way." My client is doing well, fast becoming a superstar. You never ask about her, and I never talk about my work. I never have. That fact didn't bother you until recently.

You look at me through the tower of thoughts you've constructed about us. It's a distant gaze, loaded with unresolved emotion constructed long before I came into your world.

I'm too tired to engage in another debate about my love for you.

"When are we going to have sex?" you ask abruptly.

My appetite dies. I slug my wine until the glass is empty. We've had this conversation too many times over recent months. I have no answer. I feel numb at the thought.

"It's been eighteen months."

You're the only one counting. I haven't thought about sex in a while. It doesn't occupy my mind, but it seems to consume yours. And my body switched off to you, little by little, every time you accused me of not loving you. It's not that I don't love you. I fucking love you so much, this—*us* like this—is killing me. It's a soulless existence and so far away from where we started out together. I'm protecting what little there is left of me. Not saving it for anyone else, because there will never *be* another for me. Not saving it from a broken heart, because that damage has already been inflicted. "I just don't feel like it," I say. It's the truth.

"When will you feel like it?"

At that moment, I can't think, feel, or see clearly. "I don't know."

"You don't love me. If you loved me you'd feel it."

You might be right. I don't think you are. Feelings come and go. I know my own heart. I still think I know yours.

This isn't you.

You tell me again that you need sex to feel connected.

I need to feel connected, otherwise sex feels like prostitution, I tell you. My words feel harsh even to me, and your jaw tenses. I shrug. It's how I feel, and I can't deny it. I've never been good with make-up sex, and I've always been honest with you about how I feel. You should know me, you were my therapist, right? I'm being facetious about you being my therapist I know, because it suits my argument. Making up from where we're at now would be like trying to hit the moon with a double-barrelled shotgun: futile and delusional to even try.

"You're seeking the feeling we had when we first got together," I say.

Your eyes give away the fact that you know exactly what I'm talking about. You deny it. I know I'm right. Who wouldn't want to feel that good?

I also believe sex is sex. It's the thrill, the stress relief, the insecurity gap temporarily filled. I'm adamant on this point. We are stuck.

But we had something special.

We experienced that place of absolute and total trust. In the absence of ego, we came together as one. There's nothing more powerful, more defining of the deepest kind of love than that.

I think intimacy has many levels, and the smallest things we do for each other are the ones that matter. I believe gratitude underpins our ability to value those small things and grow them into something beautiful. I tell you this, and you agree.

I want to tell you that the addict wants more and isn't free to embrace gratitude, and you can't feel connected when the guards are defending the hurt you've essentially inflicted on yourself. Tell me about your fear of commitment, my love. You have too much to lose, don't you? Too many rejections are burrowed deep in your heart that you cannot trust. Connection becomes the illusion. Sexual gratification is the cloak clinging onto the attachment that endures. Fuck that.

I watch the anger subside behind your eyes. It slips into your throat and forms a tight ball that you'll swallow down where your stomach will try to break it up into digestible pieces. Stomachs can't do that with feelings though. They throw it all back up. With interest as well as bile. I know what the future holds. I *don't* know when you'll launch the next assault.

*

I would have asked you to see someone then, get professional help, but I knew that would tap your deficiency buttons. I wouldn't do that to you. I still, genuinely, don't know what I've done wrong. I don't even know how we've come to this point. I've been doing my research though. Did you know that mental health issues can be very difficult to diagnose? I think they're impossible to live with. I think I'm on the spectrum.

I don't believe we are broken.

We're just going through a phase as all relationships do. It's been really fucking tough for us. You've been through the wringer with the hormone therapy. We've endured a lot, and we don't have a support network to call upon as many of your friends do.

They're ex-friends now, of course, and your parents are also part of the problem so we can't call on their help. My telling you this sets off another Hiroshima, only this one is in our back garden, and the fall out is drowning us both. You don't like your parents, but you resent me more for commenting on their dysfunctional attitude. And you think sex is the answer, I want to ask.

"What are you hiding from?" I ask you softly instead, as the dust settles on the scorched lawn.

Your teeth are still gritted, your lips form a perfect line as fine as the one I am clearly treading. You don't like being challenged. I've lived with you long enough to know that. But I'm trying to save our relationship and to do that, we need to be honest. "What do you want from me?"

"I want you to love me," you say.

"I do fucking love you." Despondency doesn't come close to describing how I'm feeling right now. The hamster on the revolving wheel who doesn't know how to get off is in a better place than me. I'm exhausted, drained, devoid of solutions. "I'd have sex with you if I thought it would change things, but we've been there before, and you didn't find the feeling you were seeking then, did you?" My voice rises. I don't give a shit if the neighbours can hear us.

You do.

"Lower your voice," you say, looking around and over the fences. "I feel better having sex than not. What's so bad about that?"

"So, you'd be happy for me to prostitute myself by having sex with you for an outcome you know won't change anything between us?" That isn't love. That's possession.

That's addiction. I'm fucking livid, and I say things that I think I should probably have kept to myself.

You're hurt.

I'm devastated.

Revenge is never sweet, and I haven't spat out the words to hurt you because you hurt me. Not intentionally. I want us to be together and to do that, we need to change. Together. We need to stop the wheel from turning.

"What are you running from?"

You shake your head and silent tears slide onto your cheeks.

Every ounce of me wants to pull you into my arms, hold you, comfort you, take the pain away. But I'm frozen inside, and that keeps me from doing any of those things for you. I watch the destruction unfolding within you, another level of the tower has fallen.

You are strong though, stubborn. You're not done with fighting yet.

When did I become the battle, my love? I'm not the enemy.

I go to bed with an empty heart. It's not a feeling I like at all. It's an alien invasion that leaves me devoid, but I know it will pass. The trip to Germany will help.

14.

"Hey."

"Hey," you say.

"How are you?"

"Good. I've decorated the bedroom. It looks fab."

"That's nice."

"How's Germany?"

"Good." I'm not being deliberately evasive. I'm relieved that you sound upbeat, alive, enthused. "I look forward to seeing the room."

"I miss you."

My heart does the strangest thing. It skips in anticipation of the end of the war, then immediately dives for cover. I don't miss you. At least, not in the sense of missing the life we're existing in. There's tenderness in our tone when we talk over the phone, and that gives me hope. I think it's because there are no physical cues to kick off the negativity we've anchored to our face-to-face conversations. It's good, I think, but you don't like the physical distance. I'd rather have the distance and be able to talk to you. "I miss us," I say.

When I arrive home, you *are* different. I wasn't expecting that.

"You have a new perfume?"

"Yes. Do you like it?"

I nod.

There's a faint sparkle in your eyes that holds my attention, reminds me of the early days of us, and it elicits a coy smile. The scent on you is mellow. It's pleasant. My defences hadn't fully processed the latest instructions to stand down and when you approach me, I flinch.

"What's wrong with you?"

You're pissed at me. I've been away, and you're trying to get close. "Sorry, I'm tired." It's the truth.

The light in your eyes dims, and your guards instinctively resume their well-rehearsed positions at the gate to your heart.

This has become our dance, hasn't it?

I caused that flicker of pain in your eyes, didn't I?

I'm so fucking fatigued. Not just from the hours I've needed to work, but from this destructive cycle. We've both become a hamster that hasn't just forgotten how to get off the wheel, it's forgotten it has a choice to get off.

Running is an option. I must jump off the wheel. I think you do too.

I step toward you and pull you into my arms. You yield to my embrace and lean into my shoulder. You feel as soft as you did the first time I held you to my chest after you'd walked out on *her.* The warmth of you melts the tension I walked in with. Even my heart is peeking out from behind the covers. Optimism tastes like sweet cherries as I kiss the top of your head, breathe in the new scent of you. "I like your new perfume. I'm sorry," I whisper.

You ease away slowly, gaze into my eyes.

Your sadness stings, awakens my spirit, and opens my heart to you. "We need to talk," I say.

Your smile is as sweet as it ever was. Is that agreement in your eyes or acquiescence?

"I have to go to class," you say.

I nod. Disappointment dampens the light I'd allowed in. In that sweet moment, I felt the essence of you in the softness in me.

You're distracted with your plans for the evening and the moment is lost, along with the others that have passed us by over the years of us getting to this point. You throw on your boots, cast me a fleeting glance and a tight-lipped smile, and when you close the door behind you, I feel your absence in the empty chill, the pained silence that remains.

It's only after you leave that it occurs to me it's coming up for our seven-year anniversary. Have you given up on us?

I sit in the darkness, allowing my thoughts to stream.

Is this us?

Is this our life together, till death us do part? Did I ever have a vision of our future? Did you?

Yes, I had a dream once. You did too. The Grand Canyon was on my list. The Iguazu Falls was on yours.

In my dream, we're stood at the top of the canyon, looking into the abyss that is too vast for our tiny minds to fully comprehend. Snowflakes are falling onto our jackets and coating our hair. My teeth are chattering, though I feel warm in the comfort of you. We overhear someone in the group walking past us saying that it's over a hundred degrees down there.

"That's mind-blowingly awesome," I say.

You squeeze your arm in mine and snuggle deeper into my shoulder.

"Incredible."

I can't even make out the slow-moving dots, in T-shirts and shorts probably, as they navigate their way to the thin, wavy, mud-brown line that will become a raging torrent to them another hour into their descent.

You want to take a helicopter ride. It's another level of awesomeness, and my heart is in my throat. I'm blinded by the expansiveness of the giant crater that splits the earth in two, the beauty is beyond my comprehension. I have no words to describe it. I still get as airsick as I did in 'copters in the military though.

You squeeze my hand, and there's tenderness in your eyes as you study me.

"You look pale," you say.

Your voice is gentle and you cup my cheek. I nod, turn away, and focus on the furthest point on the horizon.

You understand.

And then we're standing, staring silently at the Iguazu Falls. The noise is deafening. There's no space for words here. The spray spans for what feels like miles. It's raining waterfall, I want to scream. I squeeze your hand. Pure joy looks good on you. You look like you belong in this place. It's a dream come true for us both.

We sit in our hotel later that evening, sipping our drinks, ears ringing, hearts still racing, and our minds inspired. We have no words to describe the feeling that bathes us. Awesome just doesn't cut it. I see the falls lingering in your mind's eye, as you too can recall the canyon etched in mine.

The waiter must have overheard us talking.

"Which did you like best?"

He's the child who wants to put our experiences into a category, elevate one in status in favour of the other. In doing so, something is always lost, I think. You simply cannot compare beauty with beauty. Neither of us can give him an answer. We smile at each other. We were equally moved by both experiences. We faced the reality of our miniscule existence—a speck on a speck—in the face of the incomprehensible vastness of those magnificent wonders. Nothing can compare. There are other places that we want to explore.

You love nature. You rescued a baby hedgehog the other day. It's not the first animal you've saved. Baby birds have fallen every year from their nest in our shed roof in spring. And every year you've constructed a box, filled it with straw and cotton wool, and levered the tiny bird into it without touching it.

"The mother may start feeding it," you always say.

The birds have never survived but that won't stop you trying again next year.

"I think that little guy has got half a chance," I say. You've built a cage for him, named him Prickles, of course.

"Yes," you say and smile at me. "Boris needs a playmate."

Boris is our golden retriever. He's still a pup.

I laugh. "He'll eat Prickles for breakfast."

You mock offense. You're very protective of Boris and Prickles.

We have a cat too, and the salt-water fish tank is growing.

Our new neighbours come around for a barbeque in the evening. They haven't long moved in. They seem like nice people. They're interesting enough. He's a teacher at the local school, and she's a wine buyer for a large supermarket chain. We could see they were young lovers. She had that starry-gaze look in her eyes, snuggled tightly into his shoulder, and sought his approval from him as she spoke. He, the protector, smiled at her. They're not used to being around lesbians. You roll your eyes as you look at me. It was a cheeky gesture about them, because your smile was kind and compassionate. We were once like them.

"How long have you guys been together?" he asks.

You look at me with loving warmth. Tenderness comes through in the tone of your voice too. "It's our twenty-year anniversary next month," you say.

"Wow," she says.

She sounded horrified and we chuckled.

"That's like a lifetime," she says.

I love her directness. She reminds me of me. "You should have seen us after seven years," I say.

She frowns at me. He wants to know more. We talk to them about relationships not always being smooth sailing. But if you love each other, you'll make it work. She's adamant that won't ever happen to them. They're solid together. He's nodding. I think he agrees with us. I hope they don't separate in a few years. They look good together, and I think they'll become our friends.

We get to talking to them about our love of wine. She's a connoisseur and has been to Napa Valley, the Cape Region in South Africa, and Bordeaux in France. It's fun talking with them. We add the locations to our list of places to visit, just to sample the wine. You've always wanted to buy a vineyard in the south of France. I think it's a great idea. We both need the feeling of the sun our bones and the weightlessness of swimming in the warm seas. The all-year around outdoor lifestyle suits us, and we both detest the cold dark nights that come with winter.

We're the same, like that.

You tell them about your parents' place in the Caribbean close to the beach, their other rental in a picturesque village in central Spain with views of the mountains. They're both great holiday destinations, and we tell them to let you know if they might be interested in a cheap break. They seem excited. You say you'll ask your mum and dad on their behalf.

You're closer to your mum and dad than you've ever been. You talk as an adult to them now. Though the frequency of their calls has declined, it's you who has changed beyond all recognition, and you've taken them with you on your journey. They even talk to me now.

You severed the umbilical cord, you see. It had to happen that way. You felt it as if a switch that went off, you told me. I felt it in your emotional stability and increasing confidence, though I didn't tell you that. You stopped self-medicating. That was a big indicator. You respect them still, of course, but you don't get sucked into their unwitting destruction of you. You've claimed your power back.

You are free. Now, you can breathe.

Now you can be *you*.

I'm so proud of you for achieving that. I did it, and I'm growing more in love with *you* every day. I didn't know that was possible.

You talk to the neighbours about your work over the burgers and sausages you're cooking and how you've found your passion and your client list is growing. I love watching you when you're so enthused. Your excitement reminds me of the first time I met you. They want to know more about colour boards and design options, because they're redecorating their living room. You tell them about your new project. Our renovation is in full flow, and you have the tradespeople eating out of your hand. You're good at negotiating a deal for us, aren't you?

I talk to them briefly about my work. I'm consulting, part-time, and government is my main client. It's resulted in less travelling, and when I go away it's for a short time when I'm asked to speak at global conferences for the defence industry. It is what it is. Work has never been my life, and I'm planning an early retirement as soon as you find us that vineyard to buy. He wants me to go and speak at his school. I think that could be interesting, though I confess to you later that the thought of it is more frightening than talking to a group of senior political and military leaders.

You come to London to sign off the renovation project. We meet in the park, and you stand on the bridge with me, overlooking the river holding my hand. I don't need to ask you if you remember, of course you do. You never forgot.

You are looking at *me*.

It's one of those rare moments when I don't have a clue what you're thinking.

You take in a deep breath. The breeze dances softly in your hair. Your eyes convey tenderness. They hold me, caress me. And then your smile arrests me.

"I'm sorry," you say.

That word reaches into my heart and tears blur my vision. I'm not feeling sad. I don't need an apology, you know that about me. It's exquisite though, because you feel it. You understand the power of owning yourself. I feel my pulse quicken, and it's hurling me toward you.

I reach up and cup your soft cheek. We're both older now, but your skin tingles at my fingertips and raises the hairs at the back of my neck. "I'm sorry too. I never meant to hurt you."

You nod. You see me.

You are even more beautiful than I have ever known. You look at me and love radiates from you.

That love is for me. You feel my love too, don't you? Deeply?

We hold hands, amble through the park to our newly refurbished flat. It's just a stone's throw from my old place, bigger, and with a small courtyard garden that you have had landscaped. You would have brought Pickles with you, but we're only staying one night this time around.

I'm stunned into silence as you show me around. It's easy to see why you won an award for the interior design. It's striking. I'm so proud of you.

You run hot water into the free-standing bathtub. I pour our drinks into the classically styled crystal glasses. Chilled Chablis for you, JD for me. It's been a while since I drank JD. The memory filters through me like a shower of flickering lights.

The scent of my body wash catches in my throat, and the thought of it on you broadens the smile that is a permanent feature. We laugh a lot now. It's nice. It's the way things should be. You've got Sade's *Diamond Life* running through your phone. It's still one of my favourite all-time albums.

I lean against the door frame and smile at the way you're staring at me. *Smooth Operator*. I really can't sing, can I? I hand over the glass and watch you savouring your drink. I sip my own.

When you look at me now your heart is always open, and your mind is always quiet. It's been this way for a few years now, and I know it's not going to change.

You are with me.

"Are you coming in?" you ask.

I put my glass on the side of the bath, strip from my clothes, and join you. You part your legs so I can sit. I want to face you. I want to study you, to capture us. You leave me breathless, you see. You always have. That feeling touches you too, because your gaze falters and you clear your throat before taking another sip of your wine.

This is *me*.

This is *you*.

This is *us*.

"I love you so much," I whisper as we slide beneath the quilt after supper.

"I know," you say.

You snuggle into my shoulder and wrap an arm across my waist. Your breath is warm against my ear.

"I've found the perfect vineyard for us," you whisper.

My smile spreads through me, delivering a warm wave that passes through to you. "That's awesome." No doubt you'll talk me through the details in the morning.

"Goodnight, Claire."

"Goodnight, my love."

I wake in the aura of my dreams at the sound of a car stopping and the door slamming shut in the driveway. I've always been a light sleeper. It'll get worse the older I get, I've been told.

The front door clicks open, and your boots pound the boards as you enter the dark room. You don't see me until I stand.

You jump, hold your hand to your chest, and curse me.

In the residual feeling from my dream, your reaction makes me laugh. "Sorry, I didn't mean to scare you. How was the lesson?"

"Good."

You smell the same as you did when you went out, though the scent of the perfume has faded. It's more pleasant with time, I think. When your lips close around mine, heat bolts though me. My cynic, the one that thought you might be feeling the seven-year-itch and heading for an affair, silences. Still, this doesn't feel as sincere as it did a moment ago in my dream. I try to focus on the softness of your lips, your tongue in my mouth, teasing me, tempting me.

What happens next is an involuntary response. It's an outcome of the history we have constructed over the last few years, not the one we aspired to achieve in the future. I know it as I watch myself in slow motion, listen to the truth that flows freely from my mouth.

"I can't do this anymore, Justine." I'm referring to the hamster on the wheel, of course, but I haven't expressed myself anywhere near well enough. I'm still reeling in the blissful vision of us that has kept me company this evening.

You step back, and your body stiffens. Incredulity flames in the squinting gaze you assess me with before you voice the suspicions that have haunted you for a while.

"You're having an affair with that fucking client of yours, I know you are."

You don't even ask. You tell me categorically what I've been doing. And you couldn't be more wrong if you'd got a degree in wrongness. Reverie collides with reality. Confusion. Chaos. The final explosion that brings the tower down has just been triggered. I'm shaking my head trying to clear my mind of the debris, stop the mortar from deafening my thoughts. You're pushing me beyond my limits. My training didn't take me this far.

"I knew you were."

Your eyes are wild, vicious in their resolve. Do you really believe I would do that? Really?

Hang on. How long have you been thinking I'm having an affair with my client? Anger, meet raw pain. Hello, insanity. I'm drowning.

Were you trying to elicit jealousy in me earlier, with the new perfume? Was this some kind of test you felt you needed to put me through, for me to prove my love to you? Is this projection? Were you really thinking of taking a lover?

In your mind, I have to be the one having an affair, don't I? I'm not going to remind you that it was you having the affair with me. I'm not going to get into another conversation about the fact that I don't need the attention of people in the same way you do. That will just end in a tit-for-tat argument again. I'm done with that. I'm done with this.

You're pointing your finger in my face and shouting.

I can't hear you through my reasoning.

You stride to the kitchen, pour a large glass of wine, and drink it in one hit.

"Please, don't do this, Justine." I'm begging.

"I'm not doing anything."

You are insistent.

I am broken.

The vision, our dream of a future together, it came to me, filled me with our potential. I cannot deny that I still believe in us. If I renounce us now, we're history.

Yet I cannot take these accusations any more, my love. I can't take the blame, the suspicion, the insecurity. I'm not willing to be in a relationship with you, with us like this. I'm not willing to live in a future dictated by your past. A past that never involved me.

I am not the enemy.

It's the final truth that drives the excruciatingly painful stake through my heart. It is the one that surrenders your hold over me. My tower is down. Yours is yet to fall completely. I can't help you to bring it down now. You must make your choice. The past, the pain, or our future together?

I didn't expect my love for you to become stronger after that final act of destruction. I didn't expect the dream of our future to imprint itself in my soul. When I come back to my senses though, I see you, and I know what I need to do.

I grab your hands. You try to resist, but I'm stronger. "Please, Justine? This is not you."

"Fuck off. Fuck off. Let me go."

Your words lack conviction. Your walls are crumbling, and I'm not letting you go until you let them fall completely. I'm staring into your eyes, silently pleading with you to look at me. *See me.* I know you can. You see my love for you.

"This is not you," I repeat the words slowly, insistently.

I don't know where the calmness came from, but I'm grateful for it because it helps me think straight. I'm not letting you off the hook with my gaze either.

"If we don't grip this now, we're history," I say.

You look like you've been caught in the headlights.

"I don't have the energy to fight you anymore. I know I can't make you happy, God knows, I've tried. I'll never stop loving you, Justine. Never. I love you so much."

You know it's the truth.

You're defeated.

I watch the hostility drain from you, and when I let your hands go they hang limp at your side.

We sleep in separate rooms. The towers have fallen.

15.

We walk hand in hand across the street to the coffee shop, the one that serves the cheap coffee. We've been there so many times before, stared at each other across the space that's too narrow to deflect or defuse our shared pain. This time we sit at another table and gain a different aspect on the quaint café.

A switch has been flicked, the lightning surge has ceased.

Battle worn, resignation, this isn't a defeat.

It's the rebirth.

Something more powerful than we could image has happened, and our life, our future, together is about to begin.

Our dreams will become reality.

I sense it in the slither of an opening of my heart, the vulnerability in your forlorn eyes.

You can't hurt me anymore, because I have the courage to leave you. I can't hurt you, because you don't fear losing me. Separation isn't what I want for us. It's not what you want either. We agreed on that last night. Maybe that's what has changed.

We're both raw. The coffee has a hint of caramel in it. We both comment at the same time and then smile. There's tenderness in your gaze. I know you can feel my love for you in the way I'm looking at you, too.

When you're sat on the precipice looking into the abyss beneath you, the enemy fast approaching, knowing you must jump is the worst feeling of all. Falling is the release. Trust is the cushion that saves you and helps you land softly.

"Will you jump with me? Will you trust me, trust in us, Justine? I'm not perfect."

You cover my hand with yours. The warmth of you stops me talking.

And when I take your hand in mine, squeeze it softly, I'm standing on the bridge in the park in London again, overlooking the river. It's that split second before our lips met for the first time. The essence of you is in me, and I feel it in the adrenaline that still pumps life through my veins. My heart races now, as it did back then.

I think you feel a flicker of something from that time too, because the fine lines appear at the edges of your eyes as they narrow, and your soft smile overcomes the weariness you've endured these past years. You look momentarily rejuvenated.

"I'll go and see someone," you say.

I nod. "So will I," I whisper.

Satisfaction moves through me in a wave of relief that lightens the burden I feel I've carried for us. I know how hard this is for you. That you have conceded to the help of another professional is courageous and a demonstration of your commitment to us. Giddiness comes to me with hope. Our future together, the dreams we spoke of are being crafted in the reality of this moment, and there's no going back.

"I will talk more and be more sensitive to your needs."

You gaze at me with a look that tells me your heart never betrayed us. Your mind has reached the peak of exhaustion. It's lost the fight. Therapy will help you to let go of the battle that was never even yours.

"Will you talk to her about your childhood?"

It's always been a moot point between us. A well-guarded secret you've needed to maintain. I've never pressed you to talk to me about what happened, some things really don't need to be shared. I think it's too easy to lose your identity in a relationship where every detail about everything is the business of everyone. I exaggerate sometimes, but you know that about me now. Common interests, values, and beliefs are all important, but there must be room for independent thought. It's not about keeping secrets from each other, it's about boundaries. Privacy.

I would say that though, because this is me.

I will talk to my therapist about that. I respect the need for silence as I do the need to discuss. It's about context and intention. You need to do what is right for you. I agree to accept the consequences of your decision, whatever that means for you and for us. Because, I love you.

I have no fight with you. I am not the enemy.

"Yes."

Your voice is a whisper when you answer my question, but there is an undeniable charge behind the word.

I nod and take a deep breath. I'm happy for you. "Good."

129

Your hand is trembling in mine. Mine is shaking too. I stare into your eyes, and I see something I haven't seen there before.

Trust.

This is the real point of no return for us. We have lived through the dark night of the soul.

I smile.

You smile.

I nod.

You nod.

You know it.

I know it.

We have just jumped off the cliff together and into the abyss...into us.

This is us.

This is you.

This is me.

About Emma Nichols

Emma Nichols lives in Buckinghamshire with her partner and two children. She served for 12 years in the British Army, studied Psychology, and published several non-fiction books under another name, before dipping her toes into the world of lesbian fiction.

You can contact Emma through her website and social media:

www.emmanicholsauthor.com
www.facebook.com/EmmaNicholsAuthor
www.twitter.com/ENichols_Author

And do please leave a review if you enjoyed this book. Reviews really help independent authors to promote their work. Thank you.

Other Books by Emma Nichols

Visit **getbook.at/TheVincentiSeries** to discover The Vincenti Series: Finding You, Remember Us and The Hangover.

Visit **getbook.at/ForbiddenBook** to start reading **Forbidden**

Visit **getbook.at/Ariana** to delve into the bestselling summer lesbian romance Ariana.

Visit **viewbook.at/Madeleine** to be transported to post-WW2 France and a timeless lesbian romance.

Visit **getbook.at/SummerFate** and **viewbook.at/BlindFaith** to enjoy the Duckton-by-Dale lesbian romcom novels.

Thanks for reading and supporting!

What's Your Story?

Global Wordsmiths, CIC, provides an all-encompassing service for all writers, ranging from basic proofreading and cover design to development editing, typesetting, and eBook services. A major part of our work is charity and community focused, delivering writing projects to under-served and under-represented groups across Nottinghamshire, giving voice to the voiceless and visibility to the unseen.

To learn more about what we offer, visit: www.globalwords.co.uk

A selection of books by Global Words Press:
Aventuras en México: Farmilo Primary School
Life's Whispers: Journeys to the Hospice
Defining Moments: Stories from a Place of Recovery
World At War: Farmilo Primary School
Times Past: Young at Heart with AGE UK
In Different Shoes: Stories of Trans Lives
Patriotic Voices: Stories of Service
From Surviving to Thriving: Reclaiming Our Voices
Don't Look Back, You're Not Going That Way

Self-published authors working with Global Wordsmiths:
John Parsons
Dee Griffiths and Ali Holah
Karen Klyne
Ray Martin
Emma Nichols
Valden Bush
Simon Smalley

Printed in Poland
by Amazon Fulfillment
Poland Sp. z o.o., Wrocław